LC

Bad Boys of Hockey

- A Fake Boyfriend Sports Romance -

VIOLETTE PARADIS

This is a work of fiction. All characters and events reside solely in the author's imagination, and any resemblance to actual people, alive or dead, is purely coincidental.

This title contains mature themes and strong language.

Cover image licensing from Deposit Photos.

Bad Boys of Hockey

Logan

Jack

Rory

Cooper

Verona

Dean

Austin

Although these novels can be read as standalone stories, reading them in the above order will give you a fuller experience.

Dedicated to everyone who supported my writing dreams.

1

LOGAN

"Alright team, here's who's starting tonight. Beechwood!" The guys in the packed locker room cheer. "Jaro!" Another cheer.

The Cleveland Crushers are dressed and ready for that night's outdoor game. The excitement in the room is palpable. Coop, my best friend since childhood, leans over to me. His blond hair falls into his green eyes.

"You gonna score tonight?"

He asks.

"Only if you play well enough to set me up." I smirk.

"Oh, so you're saying you can't do it without me?"

I playfully punch him in the shoulder.

"Drake!" Coach Brauer calls my name. The team cheers. "Cooper!" Another cheer.

I pat Coop on the back. "I bet we can score in the first minute."

"Let's do it." He holds up his hand and I give him a double high-five, the way we used to when we were kids. "But I'll get the goal and the two points that go with it."

I laugh. "Oh, is that how it is?"

"Race to the Corazon trophy, right?"

"If you want to play that way, it's on."

Coach's voice fills the room as he announces the starting goalie for the night. Everyone cheers. "Now let's have a great game, guys. I know the visibility will be low since we're outside, it's snowing, and the lights will cause a lot of glare, but this is our night. Make this a night to remember! Make Cleveland proud! Go Crushers!"

"Go Crushers!" Everyone cheers again as they get to their feet and start filing out of the locker room. Everyone's chatting excitedly about tonight's outdoor game.

"Isn't this crazy?" I ask. "We've been dreaming about playing in the Ice Classic since we were kids and now it's really happening!"

"Absolutely mental. We did it."

"Come on." I stand up on my skates, towering over Coop. "Let's do this."

Coop's phone lights up in his locker.

"Don't wait up for me," he says as he grabs his phone.

Following the rest of the team outside, I marvel at the large outdoor ice rink. The sky is dark, allowing the cool air to sweep up off the ice into the air like icy fog. The stands are filled with tens of thousands of spectators all bundled up and excited for the game. The air is electric.

As I step onto the ice, icy crystals instantly start settling on my skin. I breathe in the frozen air, that smell of winter. I'm home.

"Hockey fans, welcome to this year's Ice Classic! Now if you'd all rise for the singing of our national anthem."

Skating to the center of the ice, I face the flag for the national anthem. When it's done, I look over at Coop who's glaring at me.

Whoa, why does he look so angry?

"What's wrong?" I mouth.

"You're a fucking asshole," he hisses.

What the hell?

We were fine a few minutes ago. Is this because of our friendly competition? Nothing about his expression seems friendly. There's no time to ask because the game is about to start.

We skate to our starting positions. I'm in the center circle with Coop on my left. He's still glaring at me.

"What did I do?" I mouth again, even though I should be focusing on the player in front of me and the puck that's about to drop.

He makes a gesture that I know all too well. He wants to fight.

What the fuck?

He's never acted like this before, not in the fifteen years I've known him.

The referee drops the puck while Coop and I drop our gloves. The stadium erupts into excitement and confusion as everyone rises to their feet. All I'm focused on is Coop and that snarl on his face. Before I know it, he smashes into me and I elbow him in the face. We struggle with each other while our teammates and the referees work hard to pull us apart.

"What the hell, buddy?" I manage to yell at him as I fight him off. "What the fuck are you doing?"

"You're an asshole," he spits.

The team finally pulls us apart but Coop continues to yell at me.

"An asshole!"

I feel blood dribbling out of my nose and into my mouth. The crowd is on their feet, simultaneously cheering and booing. I look around at all the lights, the cameras, and my teammates staring at me.

What the hell just happened?

***

"Absolutely embarrassing," Mr. Chapman says. The owner of the Cleveland Crushers is sitting behind his desk in his office while Coach Brauer stands next to him. I'm sitting across from them as I hold an ice pack to my face.

"Where's Coop?" My voice sounds nasal because of the bandage over my bloody nose. "I gotta talk to him."

"Harrison is still in the hospital because he had to get stitches. And just when I thought it couldn't get worse, this happens." He holds up his phone. There's a picture of me and a woman I slept with a few weeks ago.

"What the hell…" I say.

"Who is that?" Chapman asks.

"Umm…Chelsea? No, Catherine!"

"It's Cooper's girlfriend!" He says.

"Cooper had a girlfriend?"

"He was at the Christmas party with her. He said they just started dating."

"I wasn't at the Christmas party." I look around in bewilderment.

"We know," Chapman says, a tinge of disappointment in his voice.

"Does it matter? She was single when I met her…"

"That's not what she says in this article."

"She spoke to the press?" I squint at the screen in confusion. "This is a set up! She probably got paid by those stupid tabloids to lie."

Chapman shakes his head and sighs. "I think it's best if you guys take some time apart."

"Take some time apart? But we play together!"

"Not anymore."

"What?" I look at Coach. "What does he mean, Coach?"

"One of you guys has gotta go," Coach Brauer says in a soft voice. "Chapman thinks it should be you."

"Me? But I'm the third highest goal-scorer in the league this season *and* I have the highest points overall! I could be this year's MVP!"

"I know," Coach says in a dejected voice. "But it's not my decision."

"It's mine." Chapman looks up from under his glasses. "You've embarrassed us at the Ice Classic. This is one of the biggest games of the year! Do you know how hard we had to work to get this?"

"But he started it!"

"That's not what it looked like to me or any of the cameras or the millions of people watching."

"I swear!" I groan in frustration.

"This isn't the first time this happened… remember those nude photos of you that were all over the magazines last month?"

"I had nothing to do with that either! It's these women that I meet at the clubs… they take photos of me and try to blackmail me!"

"No more excuses. You're off the team. You'll be on a new team by the end of the week so I suggest you start packing."

"But I've never played without Cooper! We've been playing since we were kids!"

"Yeah, well you shoulda thought of that before you fucked it all up."

"I didn't…" I exhale angrily. "Whatever. I'll get on that new team and I'll be so good, I'll win the Corazon trophy. You guys will regret this."

Chapman looks up at me from under his glasses. "You're lucky you're even still in this league, kid."

2

RILEY

After a long three hours of class followed by three hours in the lab, I make my way up the stairs to my dorm room. Even though I still have several hours of homework to do, all I want to do is pass out in bed.

One day, I tell myself, *one day I'll graduate and finally have time for a life.* I touch the rose pendant on my necklace, my good luck charm. Hopefully soon.

I push my way into my room.

"It's about time you came home." Jane, my roommate, is standing in front of the full-length mirror, putting on a pair of diamond earrings. She's wearing a light pink cocktail dress and her makeup looks Instagram-worthy. Her dark wavy hair and striking blue eyes tend to capture a lot of attention on campus, but all dressed up like this she looks like a supermodel.

"Wow." I put down my backpack, realizing that I'm wearing stinky day-old clothes that make me look like I'm in a grunge band from the '90s. "You look great. Got a date tonight?"

"Something like that." She smirks.

"With the same guy as last week?"

She pulls out a silver tube of lipstick and leans into the mirror as she puts it on. "Mm-hmm."

Although we share a room, Jane and I are complete opposites. She's a social butterfly, which is fitting considering she's a media student who's always interviewing local celebrities. All my classes are in the sciences and I spend most of my time alone in a lab. Although we'd likely never hang out in the real world, it's hard not to get to know one another when we sleep ten feet away from each other. That'll be another benefit of graduating: gaining some privacy and a room to myself.

"Have you checked your phone recently?" Jane places her lipstick inside a glittery clutch.

"No. I've been at school all day." Pulling out my phone, I see multiple messages from her. "Is everything okay?"

"I need a favor." She's hopping as she pulls on a pair of black heels.

"Wait… are those Louboutins?"

"Uh-huh." She smiles wickedly. "Nice huh?"

"They're more than nice… they're art!"

Jane smiles. "At least you appreciate them. I doubt Rupert will notice them."

"Rupert?"

"About that… can you do an interview for me tonight?"

"An interview? I'm a physio student, not a media student—"

"It's easy. Just a few questions. Please?"

"Easy? Easy for you to say! You're used to that stuff."

"I've already written out all the questions. You just have to record the answers on your smartphone."

"Hold on." I narrow my eyes. "You're going on a date instead of doing school work?"

"It's not a date… Well, it is. It's complicated. I'll explain later. Please do this for me? I only need three more interviews and I'll pass this course."

Looking at my backpack, I let out a slow sigh. "I can't. I have my own work to do."

"Can't you do it tomorrow?" She puts her hands together and gives me her best puppy dog eyes. *"Please?"*

"I don't know… I should really study."

"Come on, you owe me. You haven't even paid me back for your cafeteria card."

Guilt churns in my belly. The last time I checked my account I was eighty thousand dollars in debt and sinking thanks to my outrageous tuition fees.

Jane's phone vibrates. She checks the screen and looks back at me. "So, can you do it?"

"You want me to cover for you so you can go on a date…"

"It's not really a date. It's work."

I furrow my brow. "Work? I didn't know you had a new job."

She hesitates. "I can't really tell you."

"Why not?"

She bites her lip. "Please will you do this for me without continuing this interrogation? You can borrow my car."

"Wait… you have a car?"

"Bought it last week!"

"Your new job allows you to afford that?"

"And then some."

"What the hell are you doing? And are they hiring?"

"They're *always* hiring." She gives me another one of those wicked smiles.

"Wait…" I look at her suspiciously. "What kind of place is this?"

She hesitates.

"Jane, tell me."

She sighs.

"Fine." She pulls out her phone. "But if I tell you about this, you can't tell *anyone*."

"Now I'm really worried."

"Riley." She looks at me with a pleading glare.

"Come on, you know I won't tell anyone. Who would I even tell?"

She nods as she taps her screen with her perfectly manicured fingers. The screen on her phone lights up and she clicks on an app that looks like a green circle.

"Oh." I squint. "So, it's an app?"

"It's an app called Green Light," she says. "You fill out a profile and people bid on you until you get hired as a date."

I pull back in shock. "Like a sex worker?"

"No, not like that. Everything is PG. I'm just his fake date."

"Fake date?"

"We're just pretending. It's like we're creating theater for the media. And you know how much I love to put on a show." She looks back at the mirror and flirts with her reflection.

"So, you're a media student participating in false media?"

"Talk about fake news, huh? It's great. I've been learning about the media firsthand from Rupert *and* getting a nice chunk of change in the process."

"Rupert, huh?"

She bats her eyelashes. "He's kind of a stud."

"Who is he?"

"He's an actor from England. The media there is insane and they've been harassing him about not being over his famous ex. He moved here to get away but the paparazzi followed him. He needed a boring American girlfriend or at least the appearance of one."

"Why?"

"The media only really cares when celebrities date other celebrities. The paparazzi backed off a bit when they realized he was just dating a lowly journalism student."

"I guess that makes sense," I say hesitantly, not really sure if it *does* make sense. "What do you guys do together?"

"I mainly tag along during award shows or film premieres. Tonight, we're going to an award show. It's great. I get to eat amazing meals, wear beautiful dresses, and I get ten thousand dollars a date."

"Ten thou—" I nearly choke.

"Right?" She fluffs her hair in the mirror. "I finally went to that hairdresser on Fifth that costs a fortune. Looks good, huh?"

"How am I only learning about this now?"

She shrugs. "He's not famous enough for America, I guess. And I figure the less I talk about him here on campus, the better. It's easier to keep my story straight."

"What if someone finds out?"

"No one knows, except for you." She turns and looks at me with her sharp blue eyes. "But you won't tell anyone, right?"

"Of course not!" I'm still trying to process all this. None of the physio students I know have nearly as colorful a life as Jane does. "How many other people out there need fake dates anyway?"

She shrugs. "You'd be surprised by how common it is. There are people who need to fool their family or friends, politicians or famous people who do it for good publicity, gay people who aren't out of the closet yet, that kind of stuff. All sorts of people are on this app."

"Ten thousand dollars a date," I say to myself.

She watches me with a devilish smile.

"What?" I'm caught off guard by her pointed eyebrow.

"You're thinking about doing it, aren't you?" She asks.

"No, I'm not! I'm not getting paid to be someone's fake date! It's absurd!"

She shrugs. "Your loss. I've already paid off my entire student debt."

"Wait... seriously?"

Her eyes flash. "I know you're tempted."

I shake my head. "No. This isn't for me."

"Why not? It's not like you're dating anyone in real life anyway. You can at least get some money out of it, pay your bills, rent, food, debt. I mean, considering you want to get one of those fancy internships next year, I don't think you have a lot of money coming to you any time soon. Just think of all those zeroes in your bank account."

She's right. But I'm not thinking of multiple zeroes, I just want one. If I could be debt-free, I'd be able to get a coveted internship next year. They don't pay much, but the experience is invaluable. That's the life of a millennial: bust your ass at school to get a minimum wage dream job.

Sigh.

At least if I do something like this, I wouldn't have to worry about all that student debt. The thought is extremely enticing. However, being found out and losing my chance at a career is not.

"It's too… insane," I say as I pull the textbooks out of my backpack. "Besides, I'm supposed to be focusing on school, not men."

"You know what's insane?" Jane asks as she fluffs her hair in the mirror. "Being eighty thousand dollars in debt."

"Hear, hear, sister," I mumble.

"And it's not about men. It's about money. You can't focus on your career when you're too broke to put food on the table."

Her phone buzzes again. "So, will you do this for me? If you do, I'll give you half of what I make… that's five thousand dollars."

"Oh my god, are you serious?"

"Will you do it?" Her striking blue eyes plead with mine.

Five thousand dollars would put a huge dent in my debt situation. I sigh and let go of my backpack. "Okay, fine."

"Great!"

"Who am I interviewing?"

Jane grabs a laminated VIP pass and tosses it to me. "The star of tonight's hockey game."

"Campus hockey? That could be fun." I look at the pass.

"Nope!" She chirps. "Major League."

My jaw drops. "You want me to interview professionals? Oh, I definitely can't do this." I hold the pass back out to her.

"You'll be fine. You know about hockey, right?"

"Umm…" I play dumb. "Face-offs. Hockey sticks…umm…"

Jane rolls her eyes. "I've seen you watching games in the student lounge before."

I sigh. "Fine. Yes, I know hockey. And I know the Seattle Blades."

"See? You'll do great! Follow your instincts and remember to ask Logan Drake at least one of these questions." She hands me a paper with three questions on it.

"Logan Drake?"

"He's the team's new golden boy, right? The one who's been in the news?"

"Yeah, but…"

"Ask one of those questions. And I want you to ask the star of the game a question too."

"Okay, but…"

"You'll be fine! Fuck, I'm late." Her gold watch glints in the light as she checks the time. Another new present, I'm guessing. "Don't forget to ask those questions. And remember to record everything! I need sound-bites otherwise Mr. Pearson is going to freak out on me again."

I shake my head. "I can't believe I'm doing this."

She smiles wickedly at me. "Enjoy the game."

***

After changing into freshly washed jeans and a plain black t-shirt, I make my way to the stadium. I flash my VIP pass so someone can usher me to the media box overlooking the ice. There are several other journalists already there. They've all found seats and have their journals and recording devices ready.

Feeling extremely out of place sitting up here with these big-time journalists, I take a seat next to an older man with a pointy white beard. I give him a polite smile and he acknowledges me with a curt nod.

To avoid being found out as the imposter that I am, I busy myself on my phone. I pretend I'm concentrating on something important when I'm actually looking up the Green Light app. I read through the terms and conditions and I even go as far as signing up before realizing how crazy the whole thing is and swiping it away.

Crazy Jane, I think to myself.

I instead focus all my attention on a video of a cat playing with a crow.

Before I become curious enough to reopen the app, the announcer's voice fills the stadium and introduces the team. One by one, he announces their names as they skate out onto the ice: Rory Edgar, Marcus Rock, James Cornelli, Logan Drake...

My eyes automatically fall onto Logan as he skates down the ice. Logan Drake. Number thirteen. The Seattle Blades' newest and most notorious player.

It's only been a few months since he was kicked off the Cleveland Crushers for a fight during the game. Fighting is fairly common in hockey but *not* when it's with your own teammate. Logan Drake and Harrison Cooper were a dynamic duo on the ice and best friends off of it. They could've won the Cup this year if he hadn't gotten himself kicked off the team. The rumor was that Logan slept with Harrison's girlfriend. It seemed pretty believable considering pictures of them in bed were all over the news. It wasn't the first time Logan's complicated reputation got him trouble. A month earlier his ex shared nearly nude photos of him on Instagram. His reputation is debaucherous to say the least.

The Blades picked him up to boost their position in the standings. After all, he's been a top scorer since he joined the league. Although I don't care for his drama or bad behavior, I couldn't help but join the city in excitement when news broke that he was coming to Seattle. His skills are second to no-one. And there hasn't been any drama… so far.

The puck drops and I'm focused on the players weaving around the crisp white ice. From up here, I have a bird's eye view of the game. I'm instantly entranced with the players gliding and zigzagging across the ice. They pass the puck to one another with accuracy and ease. Edgar gets a shot off. No score. The teams change players.

Number thirteen hops over the boards and onto the ice. It instantly feels like everyone is holding their breath and watching him as he works his magic.

The players skate up the ice into the offensive zone. Number forty, an older player named Marcus Rock, passes to Drake. I instinctively touch the rose pendant on my necklace. Drake fakes a shot to the left and swings around to the right… Logan scores!

The crowd erupts with cheers. Music pumps through the speakers and lights flash around the arena. The stadium shakes and is alive with electricity. I join the celebration, sharing a smile with Pointy Beard next to me.

When the puck drops, Rock wins the face-off and passes it to Drake, who skates faster than anyone else to score another goal in less than ten seconds. The crowd cheers even louder this time.

"*Incredible!*" I cheer again, drawing the attention of the journalists around me. I sheepishly sit back in my seat.

Logan skates toward the bench. The jumbo-tron focuses on his boyishly handsome face, his dark eyes—he's laughing, showing off a devilish smile.

Logan Drake, I write in my notebook. *Two goals.* And it's only been five minutes.

There's my star for the night.

3

RILEY

The game ends with a score of five to three for the Blades, with a hattrick by Logan. I follow the other reporters down the elevator to the locker room where I'll conduct the interview. I have no clue what to expect.

When we step in, the air is instantly humid. Steam is pouring in from the showers and hanging in the air. I inhale a mix of hot stifling body odor and men's deodorant.

The players are already undressing and showering. I've seen a few bare asses already. I'm trying to keep my eyes to myself but this is unlike anything I've ever witnessed before.

I can see the team captain, Rory Edgar, as he wipes the sweat off his intimidating biceps.

There's Skip McGovern, the goalie, shaking out his long red hair after pulling off his jersey.

Connor Saito, the half-Japanese phenom, is laughing with Marcus Rock about one of the goals.

And, of course, there's Logan Drake in the back corner of the locker room.

The other reporters gather around Logan Drake in the back corner of the locker room. I follow their lead as I hang in the back of the crowd. In an effort to see, I lift up onto my tiptoes and gasp. He's wearing nothing but his underwear! Another reporter notices my reaction. I quickly regain my composure.

Pointy Beard asks Logan the first question: "Why is it so easy for you to get a hattrick like you've done multiple times with the Blades so far?"

There are ten different microphones in his face. I fumble as I pull out my phone. *Dammit, I should have been more prepared than this!* As I turn on my phone, the cat and crow video I was watching earlier automatically starts playing on full volume. The sounds of the cat meowing and the crow cawing fill the locker room.

"Oh crap," I say a bit too loudly.

Logan Drake's attention shifts to me and, consequently, so does everyone else's.

"Pay no attention to me," I say as I swipe at the screen frantically, hoping to close the window, but it just keeps playing. *"Crap! Crap! Crap!"* I mumble to myself.

Finally, I manage to stop the video. Pointy Beard clears his throat and shoots me a disparaging look before looking back at Logan. Meanwhile, I'm silently praying to all the goddesses out there that nothing else goes embarrassingly wrong for me. Opening the microphone app, I press the big red record button. When I look up, I notice Logan Drake's captivating dark eyes staring straight at me.

Holy shit, he's hot.

My eyes dart in every direction in an attempt to avoid his fiery gaze but it's nigh impossible.

"Practice and hard work," he says, answering Pointy Beard's question. His voice is deep and smooth. "I keep my eye on the prize and I go for what I want. That's all it takes."

His eyes are still on me, watching. I can't tell if I've pissed him off or intrigued him. More steam tumbles out of the showers, filling the room with a humid fog. I'm starting to sweat.

Another reporter pushes forward. "Logan, there are rumors that you're aiming your sights on a specific trophy this season. Is that true?"

Logan watches me for a few more seconds before pulling away, looking at the reporter.

"If I keep this point streak going, I'll either be taking the Corazon home, or I'll be taking the cup home. I'm going far with these guys, I promise you that." He makes eye contact with me again. "You," he says. "I want to hear a question from you."

Oh shit. I swallow. *Here we go.* I realize Jane's questions are still in my pocket.

"Hi Logan, how are you?" I ask in an attempt to stall as my sweaty hand searches my pocket for the piece of paper.

"Pretty damn good after that win." He flashes his dazzling smile.

My heart is racing. "Right…"

"What is this?" An older reporter scoffs. "A blind date?" He turns back to the hockey player. "Logan, about your power play stats this past week—"

Logan holds his hand up and gives the man a dangerous stare. "The lady is speaking." He looks back at me. "Go ahead."

"Thank you." Looking down at the questions on the crumpled paper, I feel my heart racing in my chest. The once clean, crisp paper is now damp and wrinkled.

Why are my hands so sweaty?

I look back up and see Logan's lips twitch into a smirk. My cheeks burn even hotter. Avoiding his gaze again, my eyes blur looking at Jane's inane questions: *Do you think your bad boy reputation has affected your on-ice status as a player?*

Wtf? Damn, these questions are stupid, I think to myself. But if I don't get an answer, I can say goodbye to five grand.

"I don't need this," I mumble. Stuffing the paper into my pocket, I look up at Logan. "Those goals, especially the second one, were really spectacular."

Amused, he watches me. "Why, thank you."

There's that famous swagger of his.

I clear my throat. "But I noticed that you've been favoring your backhand. You also tend to favor your right side when you skate. Have you considered seeking a full body realignment for whatever injury you're recovering from?"

He furrows his brow. "Excuse me?"

"It's just a suggestion," I continue. "If you don't get one, it could be a problem in a few years."

Logan narrows his eyes but doesn't say anything.

Pointy Beard turns to me. "Do you think it'll affect his gameplay?"

The other reporters turn and watch me, waiting for my answer. Their microphones are in my face.

They're asking *me* questions now?

"Not if he gets it checked out—"

Logan Drake clears his throat, interrupting me. "That's enough questions for today."

There's a commotion as the other reporters mumble under their breath, their eyes shooting daggers at me. I look at Logan and he's glaring at me too.

Uh-oh. I messed up.

"Thanks for nothing," one reporter mumbles as he bumps into me with his shoulder. The reporters start to shuffle out of the locker-room.

"I didn't mean to," I say, but it's too late. *Great.* I've made enemies out of all the sports journalists in Seattle. My physio career is off to a wonderful start. I sigh as I decide whether I should hang back to avoid walking with the disgruntled journalists or if I should run far away from a furious Logan Drake before I embarrass myself in front of him again. Oh god, can't I just disappear?

As I busy myself stuffing my phone and Jane's questions into my purse, I realize something. *Crap.* I didn't get *any* questions answered. Jane is going to be *pissed.*

Looking around, I notice I'm the only non-player still in the locker-room.

"You shouldn't say stuff like that." A deep voice startles me. I turn to see Logan Drake still standing behind me. "If it gets around that I'm not in top shape, Coach will stop playing me. Other players will start targeting me. My stock will go down."

"I was only trying to help with that realignment stuff. I noticed you were shooting differently and I was just trying to help."

He watches me for a moment. There's a strange spark in his eye. "You were able to tell something was wrong just by the way I score?"

My cheeks instantly feel hot. "Your shooting technique has favored your backhand, meaning everything else gets twisted. Why aren't you shooting on your forehand anymore?"

He hesitates. "Is it bad?"

"It's not *bad*." I take a small step closer to him. I'm about to touch his shoulder to show him why it's a problem, but I stop when I realize he's still mostly naked. "But when you twist one part of your body, everything else twists with it. Everything's connected. It'll get worse if you don't get it checked out."

He watches me curiously. "Don't tell the other reporters any of this next time. And don't tell your paper either."

Next time?

"Don't worry," I say. "There won't be a next time."

There's that curious stare again. He narrows his beautiful brown eyes. "Who are you?"

"My name is Riley. I'm a student from the university. I'm filling in for my friend."

"So, you're a journalist student?"

"No, not really. Well, not at all. I'm filling in for my friend. It's a long story. I should go… but I didn't get a single question answered. She's going to be so angry with me, unless…" I look up at him with big eyes.

He raises his eyebrow. "You want me to answer a question for you? After all that?"

"Can you?"

He watches me with an intensity bordering on the intimate.

"Fine." He crosses his arms. "But just one." His stoic demeanor breaks for a second and a smirk shows through.

God, he's cute.

"Just one. Great. That's all I need." I fish out Jane's questions.

"And I get to ask you one back."

I stop and look up at him. "What?"

"I'll let you ask me a question as long as I get to ask one back." His dark magnetic eyes entrance me. The corners of his lips pull into a smile. Everything about him catches me off guard.

"Oh." Tucking my long hair behind my ear, I nod. "Okay."

Logan Drake is going to ask me a question… Cool, cool, cool…

"So, what's your question?" He cocks his head to the side.

There's a strange spark between us that I try to ignore. But it's nearly impossible. My cheeks are heated and my hands are shaking. *What is he going to ask me? And why am I reacting like this?*

My hands tremble as I ready my phone. I turn on the microphone app and press record. Pulling Jane's questions out, I stick to the script this time. Improvising clearly isn't my forte.

"Do you think your bad boy reputation has affected your on-ice status as a player?" As soon as the words leave my mouth, Logan's expression sours. Uh-oh. I've hit a nerve.

"Define bad-boy reputation."

"Umm, I guess she's asking about the nude photos on Instagram, the fight with Harrison Cooper, the affair with his girlfriend…"

"Are you from one of those tabloids?" His tone turns icy as he squares his shoulders in a defensive stance.

"No! I didn't want to ask about this stuff, that's why I asked you about your gameplay instead."

"Which went so well," he says in a sarcastic voice. "These rumors need to stop."

"If they're rumors, then clear them up right now." I hold up my phone. "Now's your chance to put them all to rest!"

"I didn't start that fight," he says. "If you watched the story closely, you'd know that."

"But you *did* sleep with Harrison Cooper's girlfriend?"

"She wasn't his girlfriend at the time—" Logan shakes his head. He steps closer so that I can smell the stifling sweat dripping down his body. His stature blocks out the light. "People don't know what really happened."

I look up into his eyes. "What happened?"

He shakes his head and smirks. "You already asked me a question."

"You didn't even answer it!"

"I think you've got everything you need." He pulls back.

"What about the nude photos?"

"Those girls posted them, not me."

"I'm sure your mom is very proud."

"Are you slut-shaming me?"

I'm taken aback. "No? I don't think so…"

"What I do in my personal time is my own business."

I force out a sharp sigh. "You know, this is why media makes stories up—you're unwilling to share anything!"

"If you're threatening to write a fake story about me, I can get you into deep trouble…What station do you work for again?" He looks down at my VIP badge.

Shit. Not getting the story is one thing, but getting Jane blacklisted from the journalism community would be far worse. I put my hand over my VIP badge so he can't read it.

"Are you threatening me?" I ask. "You know what? Never mind. Let me answer your question and I'll get out of here."

He shakes his head. "Not necessary. I've already got my answer."

"Wait… what was the question?" I ask this a bit too eagerly.

"Don't write about me," he says as he turns back toward his locker and grabs his towel, tying it around his waist. The muscles in his back ripple as he pulls his underwear off under the towel and I'm momentarily distracted.

"Excuse me?" I ask.

"All that stuff you recorded?" He says as he turns back around. "Delete it."

"But I need to give something to my roommate. How am I supposed to get paid?"

"That's not my problem." He walks toward the showers.

I know I should just swallow my pride and walk away, but I can't help myself. When the heat rises up inside me, it bubbles over and explodes, usually in the form of instantly-regretted words.

"I know you were going to ask me out," I say, cringing instantly.

Stupid, stupid, stupid. Why the hell did I just do that?

Logan Drake stops, turns around, and smirks.

“You really think that’s what I was going to ask?”

“Well, wasn’t it?"”

Amused, he watches me for a moment.

“I’d like to ask my question now,” he says.

“Oh,” I say, stunned. “Okay.”

“Would you have said yes?” He asks.

My heart flutters. *Fuck.*

“You have to answer,” he says. “It’s my question.”

The bad boy of hockey is asking me if I would date him. The bad boy of hockey is wearing nothing but a towel and asking me if I would date him. How do I say no?

I shake my head. “You didn’t answer my question, so therefore I’m not answering yours.”

He stares at me with the most impenetrable smirk. “Fine. I’ll answer your question if you answer mine.”

I swallow. “Fine.” I pull out my phone and hit record.

“I don’t think any reputation of mine is going to affect my status as a player. I’m going to let my statistics speak for themselves because I’m focused on what I want. And when I want something, I get it.” His dazzling brown eyes look deep into mine. “Is that what you wanted?”

I’m staring into his eyes as I nod absently. “Yes.” The word barely sounds louder than a whisper. My phone nearly slips out of my hand.

“And now it’s your turn to answer mine.” He gives me a cocky grin.

Damn. He’s good.

I hold myself up high.

“I would have said no,” I say. “Because I don’t date.”

He raises an eyebrow. “You don’t date? Or you don’t date guys like me?”

“Are you upset that I said no?”

“Women don’t usually say no to me.” He gives me a cocky smile that causes me to roll my eyes. “So, what’s the answer?”

My mouth opens and closes. I shake my head. “You already asked me a question.”

“I guess I’ll never know, then.” He gives me one last swoon-worthy smirk before turning away toward the showers. As he pulls the towel off his body, I catch a fleeting glimpse of his perfect ass before he disappears into a cloud of mist.

Several other players turn to look at me. The reality of where I am settles in, causing my cheeks to burn. Putting my phone away, I keep my gaze on the floor as I dash out of the locker room and rush home.

4

LOGAN

"Do I still have a bad boy reputation?"

I'm standing in Jay Spinner's small office while scrolling through headlines on my phone.

The round man looks up at me. "Huh? Are you Googlin' yourself, kid? Don't do that. It'll save ya a whole lotta trouble."

Jay Spinner is the team's public relations manager and is an expert when it comes to a player's public image.

"A reporter asked me about it after last night's game," I say. I think back to the beautiful blond woman with the gray sea-glass eyes.

"Well, you *did* fight your own teammate in the middle of a hockey game not too long ago. Not to mention all those nude photos. I've seen more nudes of you than my own wife, kid."

"That was two months ago! People are still talking about that?"

Spinner looks at me from under his bifocals. "Scandals are hard to forget, kid."

"Scandals." I laugh. "What a joke."

"You've gotta admit, you've been quite… er… *promiscuous*."

"I'm a young single guy. Just because I'm semi-famous doesn't mean I should get shamed for my sex life."

"Didn't you hear what I just said about the nudes?"

"That woman was blackmailing me! And god knows how much Catherine got from those tabloids."

"I think more people care about your broken friendship with Harrison."

I sigh. "If only people understood what actually happened. I hooked up with her *once*, she managed to get a nude photo of me while I was sleeping, and I guess she started dating Coop so that the photo would create as much drama and money for her as humanly possible. You believe me, don't you?"

"The truth doesn't matter. All that matters is perception, kid."

"This isn't fair! She tricked both of us, and I'm the one who had to lose my city, my team, my best friend. And now I'm saddled with the 'bad boy' title too?" I pace back and forth through the small office.

"Ignore it, kid," Spinner says casually.

"How? This is going to affect my chances of getting the Corazon trophy."

"Who told you that?"

"This woman in the locker room earlier…"

"A journalist? From where?"

"A student from the university, I think."

Spinner laughs. "University news? You've got nothin' to worry about, kid. Focus on your game and try for the Points Leader trophy instead."

"Can't I have both?" I drop down onto one of the large chairs and run my hands through my hair. "This team, these trophies, they're the only things keeping me going. They're all I have left!"

Spinner sighs and takes off his bifocals. "This isn't just about the trophies, is it?"

I look up at the ceiling. "Reporters pester me, my friends hate me, I attract all the wrong women, and—worst of all—the league thinks I'm a goon. Everyone thinks I'm a player."

"I hate to break this to ya, kid. But you kind of are."

"I don't want to be anymore. It's been months since that stupid scandal and it's still following me around. Why can't I be judged by my own merit rather than my personal life?"

Spinner sits back in his chair. "Kid, I've gotta give ya credit. I was expecting a train-wreck when you came onto this team, but you've impressed me. You're charmin', you're good-lookin', you're likeable. Yeah, you've got some rough edges—your antics with women could be better. But you're a phenom on the ice, let me tell ya. You wanna be great? You already are great."

I shake my head. "It's not enough."

"So you've got a reputation? Who cares?"

"I don't wanna *just* be great. I want to be the greatest. That's why I care. If people keep using me—if they keep dragging everything I've worked for through the mud, then what else do I have?" I drop my head into my hands. "I have the worst luck."

"It ain't luck, kid." Spinner stares at me. "If ya really want to clean this shit up, ya gotta do everything I say. Can ya do that?"

"Of course." I inch closer to the edge of my seat, leaning in towards him. "What do I have to do?"

Spinner opens his agenda and flips through a few pages. "There are a lot of team events coming up. We'll reconstruct your social life."

"My social life?"

"No more random girls at the club. If I see anything that's not family-friendly pop up on the internet, you're losin' that trophy. That means no more nude photos on Instagram."

"I have no control over what pictures those girls take when I'm asleep—"

Spinner looks up and gives me a menacing look.

"Okay, okay," I say. "No more one-night stands."

Spinner pauses and narrows one eye. "How far would you go to win that trophy?"

"I would do anything."

"Anything?"

I nod."

"This is what we'll do. We'll get ya a girlfriend. It'll erase the one-night stand image people have of you."

"Get me a—" I laugh. "Like some sort of matchmaker? No thanks." Catherine flashes through my mind. If those are the kinds of women out there, then I'd rather be single for a decade or two.

"Why not?"

"A girlfriend is the last thing I need right now. I have to focus on my training." I think back to the woman in the locker room and what she said about the full-body realignment. I've got to get my body back in peak condition.

"I know what you're thinkin', kid. I ain't talkin' 'bout a real girlfriend. I'm talking 'bout one for show."

"A fake girlfriend?" I laugh. "You want me to get a *fake* girlfriend? And this is going to fix my problems? That's the most ridiculous thing I've ever heard."

But Spinner doesn't seem to think it's ridiculous. He's taking notes and typing something into his computer.

"Everyone does it, kid."

"Everyone?"

"They just don't tell no-one. Trust me, we'll get you someone loyal—someone who won't upload a picture of your junk to Instagram. Someone who won't use you to get on the front page of the gossip rags."

I laugh. "What am I supposed to do with a fake girlfriend?"

"Hold her hand in public, bring her to every public event, have dinner every once in a while. The media will be intrigued for a week or two before getting bored."

"Do I want them to be bored?"

"Absolutely, kid. All the focus will be on your career—your goals, your plays. Don't ya wanna be judged by your achievements?" He sits back in his chair and looks at me from under his heavy brows.

"Of course I do."

"Good. And trust me, once they get bored of you they'll find someone else to villify. Do this, and as long as ya keep playin' the way you've been playin', you'll get the Corazon."

Staring at Spinner, I contemplate his suggestion. "What if the media finds out she's not actually my girlfriend? If this gets out, I'll look like a grade-A douche-bag."

"Worse than you look now?"

I pause and think about it for a moment. "Maybe."

"Listen, kid. They won't find out unless ya tell 'em."

I narrow my eyes. "Isn't there anything else I can do?"

"If ya wanna impress those judges, you need your personal life to reflect your professional life. You're hot on the ice, you gotta be hot off the ice. A superstar in every way. Unless you find a real girlfriend, this is your best choice."

"So…" He brings his hands down loudly onto his desk. "Will ya find someone on your own? Or do you want me to help ya find someone? You know what? How 'bout I just hire you someone. Your track record hasn't been the greatest, kid."

"Hey—"

But Spinner holds his hands up. "Think about it."

Over the past few years, there hasn't been a single woman who hasn't dated me for something other than fame, sex, money, bragging rights, or the simple desire to destroy my life. A one-night-stand with Catherine destroyed my relationship with my childhood friend. The woman before her uploaded nearly nude photos of me onto the internet after I refused to give her ten grand. And the woman from the locker room nearly destroyed my career with that comment about my injuries.

I shake my head. She was with the media and I still wanted to ask her out. *Am I a self-loathing psychopath?*

"Whaddaya think, kid?"

I look up at Spinner. "Here's a thought: How about I quit the one-night stands and remain the hockey league's most eligible bachelor? That way, I don't have to get into a relationship at all—real or fake. It seems like a much healthier option, doesn't it?"

Spinner shakes his head. "We're tryin' to get away from the reckless narrative, not enforce it. You need to be predictable, boring. Get a new girlfriend, fade in with the rest of the team. The judges will focus on your talent. You want that trophy, don't ya?"

I nod. "Maybe you're right. Maybe paying someone to be my fake girlfriend is the way to go." No sane woman would date me—not with my obsession with my work, and definitely not with my reputation.

Spinner points at a date on his calendar. "There's a team charity event this Saturday. I'll pick someone and send you the details." He waits for my answer. "Logan?"

Something about hiring a girlfriend sounds off but after everything that's happened over the past year, what choice do I have?

I nod. "I'm listening."

"You'll show up with a date this weekend."

I sigh. "I guess I have no other choice."

***

Driving up the hill to my penthouse suite, I think about everything Spinner said. He thinks I can't get a real girlfriend. It's ridiculous. I've always been able to bring a woman home. Sure, I've never tried to make them stay but I've never really tried.

Parking in the garage, I make my way upstairs. The house is a two-unit condo on a hill overlooking the ocean. Before heading upstairs to the penthouse suite, I knock on the door to the downstairs unit.

An old lady with white curly hair opens the door.

"Logan?" She's so small that she has to crane her neck all the way back just to make eye contact with me. Her cloudy gray eyes are made giant by her massively round glasses.

"Hey, Madeline. I got this for you." I hand her a puck. "Last night's game-winner."

"Oh, aren't you sweet!" Madeline sold me the penthouse when I moved here. She was an actress over sixty years ago and was in a string of popular movies that still pay royalties to this day. She must be making bank because this place wasn't cheap.

"Why is a young, handsome man like you still single?" She asks. Old ladies always seem to point out what a catch I am. Something about that demographic seems to be much more accepting of my "bad boy reputation" than women my age.

"Sometimes I ask myself that same question."

"I'm still waiting for you to ask me on a date."

I smile. "I couldn't handle the pressure of dating such a legendary actress."

"We'd certainly make headlines."

I laugh. "Oh, you have no idea."

I stop and consider it for a moment. How angry would Jay Spinner be if I showed up to the gala with eighty-year-old Madeline? His head would probably explode.

Madeline's frail, wrinkled hand grabs my arm and gives me a shake. "You'll find someone. Good guys like you aren't single for very long." A cat meows behind her. "Oh, damn. That's Ravioli. He sure gets cranky when he hasn't eaten yet."

"I know how he feels." I rub my stomach.

"Are you hungry? I have leftover lasagna—I know it's your favorite."

"Madeline, what would I do without you?"

She packs up a plate of lasagna for me before I head upstairs to my empty penthouse suite. Sitting in the dark at my dining room table, I turn on the TV. Sitting alone, I watch hockey highlights while eating the leftover lasagna.

5

RILEY

"So, when you say almost naked... how *almost naked* are we talking about?" Jane asks. She's sitting on her bed while I'm sitting at my desk on my laptop.

"Almost everything," I say. "I saw his ass."

"And?"

"He looked like he was carved out of marble. Broad shoulders, bulging muscles, and abs for days. He has so many abs I'm convinced even his dick has abs."

Jane laughs.

"Seriously," I say. "He was perfect. Guys like that don't exist."

"Sometimes they do. It's a good thing I wasn't there," she says. "I would've jumped that."

"Trust me, I almost did." I sigh. "Why can't I stop thinking about him?"

"Because he's hot."

That's an understatement, I think to myself. And he was kind of flirting with me, I think? Even though he kinda-sorta rejected me? I'm still so confused but I keep it to myself. There's no need to get Jane riled up and have her convince me to become another notch on his bedpost. Besides, a professional athlete like Logan Drake wouldn't date a nerd like me for very long. He never dates *anyone* for very long.

"Remind me to interview him next week," Jane says. "I want to see these dick-abs in person."

A pang of jealousy shoots through my belly. "What about your boyfriend?"

"*Fake* boyfriend. As long as I'm discreet, he doesn't care."

"Right… Just watch out with Logan."

"Why?"

"Well, for one, I think he hates the school's journalism team now."

"*Great.* Well, there goes that option."

"And… well, just listen to the files I sent you. He's not the most accommodating interviewee. There's like one and a half sentences of content, if that." I think back to the painful interview and cringe.

"That's fine," Jane says. "I did a whole report on two words once."

"Did you really?"

"They don't call me Janey Journalism for nothing."

There's a knock on the door.

She furrows her brow. "Expecting anyone?"

"No." I answer the door. A lanky guy with patches of facial hair stands in front of me. "Oh… it's you."

"Who is it?" Jane calls out.

"Keith," I say.

"Ugh."

Keith leans his lanky body into our room, peeking inside.

"Damn, I was hoping you'd both be naked. There go my fantasies!"

Jane and I exchange an annoyed look.

"Hi Keith," we both say in bored voices. I sigh. "What do you want, Keith?"

"I want you, baby." His gaze lands on me. A sick feeling turns in my stomach.

"Ugh." I close the door but he puts his foot out, blocking my attempt to close it.

"Actually…" He sticks his head into our dorm. "Jane, did you finish your blog for media class?"

"Yeah, I finished yesterday."

"Can I look at it?" He asks.

"Seriously?" Jane raises her brow. "You're just going to steal my ideas? No thanks."

"Do you want the answers for next week's quiz?"

Jane's eyes grow wide. "You have those?"

"In exchange for a peek at your blog."

"Absolutely not! Do your own work."

He rolls his eyes. "Fine. I'll go bug someone else then."

"Please do!"

I try to close the door again but his foot is still in the way.

"But seriously," he says, "I have the whole night off and I'm looking for someone to Netflix and Chill with. Mostly chill, if you catch my drift."

"No!" I try to close the door again.

He reaches into his pocket and pulls out a string of condoms. "I've got twenty of these bad boys and I'm ready to use them."

"Ew—" Jane squeals.

"Can you *please* leave?" I push him out into the hallway and join him out there, closing the door behind me so that Jane can't hear. "Can you stop bugging me?"

"I thought we had something good going on."

"No, we don't. We discussed it, remember? What we did was a one-time thing."

"Well, if we're not gonna do it again then maybe I should tell everyone what we did." He gives me a smarmy smile.

"What?" I wrinkle my nose in disgust. "Okay, well, if you do that, then I'll tell everyone it only lasted six seconds."

His eyes grow wide. "You wouldn't!"

"I really would though."

"But then you'd admit to everyone that we did it, that you like me." He smirks again.

"Not because I liked you, but because you were…"

He raises his eyebrows and smirks. "Sexy?"

"Easy," I blurt out.

"Oh." He seems hurt for all of two seconds before shrugging it off and leaning in. "Well, if you want something easy tonight—"

I put my hand up. "That won't be happening. I don't owe you anything and you don't owe me anything. This is over, okay? Go be easy with someone else."

He rolls his eyes. "Whatever. You're not even that hot anyway." He pulls away.

"You didn't think that ten seconds ago," I call out as he walks away. He disappears around the corner and I shake my head. Why did I ever let myself sleep with that guy? *Because I don't date,* I remind myself. A girl's gotta get off somehow, right? Swallowing back the regret, I go back into my dorm room.

"What was that about?" Jane asks.

"Nothing, just telling him to leave us alone."

"Good. What a creep."

"Yeah," I mumble. I sit at my desk and continue with my homework.

"I gotta go." Jane jumps off her bed and grabs her purse. "Manhattalyn and I are going to have coffee together."

"Manhattalyn?" I hold my tongue.

"Brooklyn's sister."

"Err... right."

"See you later tonight?" Jane checks her hair in the mirror.

"I'll be right here, working away as usual." I look at the tower of homework.

"You've gotta get out more, girl."

"Don't I know it," I mumble.

She disappears and I work until the sun starts to set. When I finally take a break, I pull my phone out to browse the internet for a bit. When my home screen flashes on, I see the Green Light app. I open it again and stare at the profile that I started filling out the previous day.

It'd be absolutely insane to make someone pay to go on a date with me. But on the other hand, if what Jane says is true, I'd only have to go on a handful of dates to pay off my entire student loan debt. Besides, my fake date can't be worse than Keith, right?

I'd be crazy to…

My finger lingers over the 'edit profile' button.

Desperate times call for desperate measures.

Clicking the button, I fill out the rest of my profile and select my preferences. Willing to travel? I select the Seattle area only. PDA? I look up the acronym—public displays of affection. I set that preference to 'mild', which includes hand-holding and public hugs. Price range? Now, this is a weird one. I've never had to put a price on myself before. Considering for a moment, I set the price unreasonably high, hoping that the exorbitant amount will make this all worth it.

Biting my lip as I stare at the bright green 'ACCEPT' button, I think about what I'm about to do.

I can't believe I'm considering this.

I can still back out… But I see the dollar signs shining bright, dancing naked in front of my eyes, taunting me. This is the only way I'll pay off all that debt.

Just one night, I tell myself. I can do this for one night and I'll have ten grand to put toward my student debt. That's a huge chunk of money. After that, I can cancel the app and I'll focus on graduating and applying for jobs to pay off the rest of my debt. Taking a huge breath, I push 'ACCEPT'. As I stare at the screen, I feel my heart racing in my chest.

Low-key freaking out, I throw my phone onto my bed and rub my face.

"What the fuck did I just do?"

Panicking, I spring across the room and grab my phone but before I have a chance to push 'CANCEL', a notification pops up saying I've been matched for Saturday night.

6

LOGAN

Following the directions Spinner sent to my phone, I drive to the library next to the University campus. It's a strange place to meet for a date but Spinner said that's the address my mystery date gave.

Rain is coming down and the sky is dark. As I pull along the side of the library, I see a woman holding an umbrella standing under the awning. She's wearing flats and I can see a dress under her long trench coat. That must be her. She peeks out from under her umbrella. I flash the lights and she hesitantly makes her way over.

This is ridiculous, I think to myself. But if this will clean up my image, then I have no other choice.

The car door opens and the woman looks inside. Striking pale gray eyes connect with mine. She's not wearing her glasses but I recognize those gray sea-glass eyes anywhere. *It's her.* The mystery woman from the locker room.

A flood of thoughts rush through my head: *Is this investigative journalism? Is she writing an exposé on me? But why would she do this? Who is she?*

This situation is already messy, but leaving her here and driving away won't make things better.

"So, we meet again," I say.

The color drains from her face when she recognizes who I am.

"Oh. Umm… I must have the wrong car." She pulls back.

"Riley?" I hold up my phone, showing her the information Spinner sent me. "Your name is Riley, right?"

"Shh." She looks around as if someone might recognize us. "I have no clue what you're talking about."

"Get in," I say. "Before you get too wet."

She hesitates before awkwardly collapsing her umbrella and climbing into the passenger seat. I put the car in park and face her. Her blond hair is half up, half down and although she's wearing much more makeup tonight than she was the other night, she's just as cute in a dorky kind of way. She opens her mouth to speak but closes it again. Her gaze darts down and to the side.

"Who are you?" I ask. "Jane, the student journalist from the University? Riley, my fake date? Do you have any other fake jobs I should know about?"

A sarcastic laugh escapes her lips along with the strawberry scent of her lip-balm.

"Okay," she starts, "first of all, I do not do this all the time. Or ever. This is a one-time thing. I'm not a journalist either. I did that as a favor for a friend. I'm Riley, a student majoring in biomechanics and physio.

"Biomechanics?"

"I study the movement and structure of the body."

"I could've guessed that."

"How?"

"You know a lot about muscles and movement. I figured you were in physio, or sports medicine, or something medical."

She smiles.

"What?" I ask.

"I thought you were going to say it was because I'm nerdy."

I laugh. "Well, you are a bit nerdy."

"Hey!"

"It's okay, it's cute." I flash a glance at her. She bites her smile back and looks away.

"And you?" She asks, still looking down at her hands. "Why does international hockey star Logan Drake need a fake date? You told me women don't say no to you." She looks back up.

I sink back in my seat. "I'm trying to fix my so-called 'bad boy reputation'. Some *really* unprofessional and amateur journalist asked me about it the other day and I thought she had a point."

She raises her eyebrows. "So, your solution is to hire someone to date you?"

"As soon as they see me as just another guy, they'll focus on what matters—hockey. Everything has to be perfect for me to win the Corazon trophy this season."

"The Corazon trophy?"

"It's the trophy for the most valuable player, as determined by all the hockey journalists. They vote at the end of the year, which is why I need to impress them all."

She rolls her eyes. "Here's a little insider tip." She leans in. "Fake dating isn't going to make your image any better."

"It's a good thing nobody will find out then."

"How do you know that?"

"Because I'm not going to tell anybody and neither are you."

She pauses and stares out the window at the other students walking by. Rain is starting to come down harder, trailing down the windows.

"You're right. Nobody can know I ever did this. On second thought, I should go. This was a stupid idea anyway." She places her hand on the handle.

"Wait—"

She stops. "What?"

I stare at the beautiful woman sitting next to me. It's rare for a woman to turn down a date with me (even if it's a fake date), and it's even rarer for people to turn down money. Something about her is different.

"Come to the gala with me tonight," I say.

"Seriously? You still want me to go with you? Even after I asked you that dumb question in the locker room?"

"Sure. We're already all dressed up, aren't we? Just pretend you're my girlfriend long enough to impress the journalist that's going to be there tonight, Jake Turner. Make him think I'm more than just a party guy so that he'll warm up to me. You'll get your money. Everybody wins. It's foolproof."

"It's not foolproof, it's stupid. If we get found out, it'd be a huge scandal! You'll get dragged by the press and I won't get accepted or hired anywhere. Schools and hospitals are going to search my name before they hire me, you know. The risks outweigh the benefits."

I chuckle.

"Why are you laughing?" She sits back, eyes wide and arms crossed.

"Not many people usually tell me I'm wrong."

"Well, maybe they should start!"

I smirk. "Okay, how about I write a check for double what you originally wanted."

"Holy crap, are you serious?"

I pull my checkbook out of the glove compartment.

"Yeah, why not? You need the money and I need to impress that journalist." I write the amount onto the check.

"Here." I hold it out to her. "This is yours if you help fool Turner into thinking I'm some soft, sensitive soul who always thinks twice before doing anything impulsive." I laugh. *"Yeah right."*

Her gaze moves from the check to my eyes. Her stoic expression continues to elude me.

"Come on," I say. "We'll eat good food and you can hang off the arm of the most handsome and skilled player in the league."

She rolls her eyes. "It's a good thing you're not full of yourself."

I smirk. "So, what do you think?"

Her eyes linger on the check. She exhales. "Oh boy, I can't believe I'm considering this. If this gets out—"

"It won't."

She stares at me for a moment with those stunning sea-glass eyes. "Fine, I'll do it. Under several conditions… First, no kissing."

"Got it, no kissing."

"Second, this is only a one-night thing. This fake date lasts until midnight."

"Aww, it's like our very own fairy tale."

She sends me a venomous look before continuing. "And, lastly, if this check bounces and you're lying to me, I want twice the amount in cash."

I smile. "Is that all?"

Her forehead wrinkles. "I think so."

"Great, so it's a date. Should we go, then?"

She nods hesitantly. "I can't believe I'm doing this."

"You're steaming up the windows."

"Oh." Her hands touch her cheeks. "Sorry."

I laugh. "I was referring to the rain on your clothes but it's good to know that you're blushing." I turn the air conditioning on.

She looks down at her damp coat. "I knew that."

I smirk as I put the car in drive. "Let's do this."

***

Once we arrive at the gala, I hand the keys to the valet and help Riley out of the car. We check our coats and I catch a glimpse of her in an elegant black cocktail dress. A dainty necklace with a rose pendant hangs delicately on her neck.

I reach for her hand but she pulls back abruptly.

"Oh," she says. "I didn't expect us to hold hands.

"Your rules said no kissing but there was nothing about holding hands."

"Is it necessary?"

"I just thought if we're dating, it's more believable if I'm holding your hand. That's just the type of guy I am."

"Oh. Right." She awkwardly puts her hand out and I interlace my fingers with hers.

"Are you ready?"

She nods. "As ready as one can be." She's still stiff as a board.

"You can relax, you know."

She gives me a tight smile.

Squeezing her hand, I pull her into the gala. People in suits and dresses are socializing all around us—hockey players, sponsors, politicians, journalists. Waiters are weaving in and out of the crowd, serving drinks and appetizers. A string quartet plays jazz standards in the corner.

Riley tugs on my hand, stopping me as she shrinks back.

"Is everything okay?" I ask.

"It's just… I'm not used to big crowds and parties. I spend a lot of time alone."

"Let me guess—studying?"

She gives a quick nod. She looks around the gallery but it's clear she's lost in thought.

"You were never a social kid, were you?"

Looking at me, she sharpens her gaze. "I was a very timorous child growing up."

"Tim…berous?"

"Timorous," she repeats. "It means I was a bit hesitant, fearful. I lacked confidence." She clears her throat.

"Well, on my arm, you don't have to feel that way." I give her a quick wink and instantly regret it. *Why am I like this?*

She rolls her eyes. "I guess you were never lacking in the self-confidence department."

"Not really, no. But come on, you don't have to be afraid."

"I'm not afraid. I'd just rather be studying."

"No studying," I say. "Tonight is for relaxing."

"Studying *is* relaxing. This?" She looks around at all the people chatting. "This is stressful."

I laugh. "And you were offended that I called you a bit nerdy."

"Only I'm allowed to call myself nerdy."

I smile. "Noted. Look, this doesn't have to be intimidating. Just do what I do." I let go of her hand. "Shake out your shoulders like this, then roll them back."

I shake my shoulders and she mimics my movements.

"And then stretch your neck like this." I tilt my head to one side.

She copies me, tilting her head to one side, then the other. She closes her eyes.

"Oh, that feels good," she says.

"See?" I watch as she sinks into the feeling. I can't help but admire her long, slender neck and her smooth flawless skin.

Among all the hockey players and older men in the room, Riley stands out like a peach in a pile of pineapples.

Her pale gray eyes flash up and catch me staring. Looking down and away, she leans in, bringing that sweet strawberry scent with her. "You're staring at me, Mr. Drake."

"I can't help it. You look beautiful."

Her cheeks grow pink and she averts her gaze.

"I know this is all an act," she says, "but you can tone it down when we're alone."

"I'll reign it in. It's just weird being a—" I look around and lower my voice, *"a fake couple."*

"I know. I'm not used to it either, but let's save the couple stuff for when we're actually around other people."

"Noted. Come, let's look at the paintings." I take her hand again and I can't help but notice how comfortable it fits in mine.

As we walk through the gallery, the chatter fills the room and waiters weave through the crowd with drinks. I grab two gin and tonics and hand one to Riley as we walk toward the art pieces.

"So, why biomechanics?" I ask.

"It's what my Aunt Mary did." She touches her necklace. "She was very important to me growing up. She was an incredibly smart woman who ran the biomechanics lab here at the university for twenty-five years."

"That's very impressive."

She nods. "She used technology to help a lot of people learn to walk again."

"Suddenly being a hockey player doesn't seem that impressive."

"Hockey is still impressive. Maybe not *as* impressive. But still impressive." She gives me a devilish smirk and I suddenly feel something unexpected stir deep inside me.

Pushing my thoughts aside, I clear my throat. "So once you get your degree, what do you want to do?"

"I want to work in the biomechanics lab here in Seattle, just like Aunt Mary did. As long as I make her proud, I'll be happy."

"I'm sure she's very proud of you.'

Riley gives me a tight smile. "Thanks."

I notice her hand is on her necklace again.

"Did she give you that necklace?"

Riley puts her hand down, as if not even realizing she was touching it. "Yes. She got it as a gift when she first got accepted into college. She said it was her good luck necklace. Good things happened when she wore it. She gave it to me when I graduated high school, a few months before she died.'

"I'm so sorry."

"Thanks." She gives me an awkward smile. "I never know what to say when people say that." She looks down and takes a sip of her cocktail.

"So, what happens after school?" I ask.

"I'm applying for internships this summer."

"Any preferences?"

"Somewhere here in Seattle," she says without hesitation.

"Of course. Following in Aunt Mary's footsteps."

"That's right." She smiles and for the first time all night, I see her glowing. "I've thought about moving again, the way you do, but I don' t know… It would be so nice to stay here in Seattle, in the city that Aunt Mary loved."

"Moving is exciting the first time around. After doing it several times, you start to get sick of it."

"Does that mean you're staying in Seattle for good?" There's a bit too much excitement behind her question. I smile to myself.

"I'm staying as long as the team decides to extend my contract. And as long as nobody picks a fight with me on the ice."

She laughs. "At least you can poke fun of yourself." Her gray eyes twinkle.

I can't help but smile as I watch her. We smile at each other for a few seconds too long, causing her to look away.

"So, do you like art?" She asks.

"I'm more of a sports guy."

"Really? I haven't noticed." She laughs and it feels like a light has been turned on.

"You?"

"I go to the odd museum here and there. I like this one." She points at a large painting that is split down the middle—the left half is blue and the right half is red and fiery. "I like the contrast between the two. The calm blue and the jarring red. It reminds me of the brain."

I laugh. "The brain?"

"Yeah! The left side of the brain is the cool, calm hemisphere. It deals with logic, math, facts. And the right side is the wild half—that's where creativity and imagination come in. Where passion comes from. Though they're separate, they work in harmony. It reflects the duality of life. Sometimes it's calm, sometimes it's wild. Yesterday I was a student in dirty sweatpants, now I'm at an art gala rubbing elbows with millionaires. Sometimes life is boring and other times you meet a hockey player twice in one week. Life is full of dualities like that." Her lips curl into a smile.

I admire her for a moment. "You're smart. I like that."

Her cheeks pinken but she stands tall, lifting her chin up as she looks back at the painting.

A large burly man with a beard appears next to us.

"Marcus," I say. "I want you to meet Riley. Riley, this is Marcus—"

"—Marcus Rock," she says, finishing my sentence. She gives him a rigid handshake.

I raise my eyebrows as I stare at her, surprised.

"Nice to meet you," Marcus says. He flashes me a devious glance and I instantly know that he'll grill me about her later. Although we've only really known each other for a few months, he's become my closest friend here in Seattle.

"What're you doing there, champ?" I ask, noticing the paper in his hand.

Marcus straightens up, showing off his large frame. "Bidding on paintings, what else does it look like? It's a silent auction, after all. Do you guys like this one?" He points at the red and blue painting we were just looking at.

"I love it," Riley says. She looks at me.

"Oh, me too," I add. "I like that it represents the duality life. The red and blue represent opposites, like passion and logic, you know? The wild and calm."

"Wow, man. I didn't realize you were such a poet." Marcus gives me a knowing smile. There's a look in his eye as if he knows I'm trying to impress Riley.

Meanwhile, Riley is staring at me with an annoyed glance. She gives me a playful shove.

"What?" I ask.

"You're so *annoying*," she says. "You stole my homework!"

I laugh.

Marcus holds up the piece of paper. "Do you think that's too much?"

Riley's eyes widen. "Wow!"

Marcus scratches his head. "Not enough?"

"No, that's… *a lot*."

Marcus looks down at his bid. "Oops. I've been guessing this for every painting."

"Every painting?" Riley can't hide her shock as she looks at me, then back to Marcus. "What if you win them all?"

"Then I'll have a really decorated apartment, I guess." He laughs, then pauses as realization dawns on his face. "Shit, I really didn't think this through."

I laugh. "Oh, boy. Better go talk to someone, buddy."

"Yeah… I'll catch you two later." Marcus disappears.

I turn to Riley. "He's great on the ice. Not so smart off of it."

"He's much taller in real life than I expected," she says.

"Wait, does that mean I'm not as tall as you expected?"

She shrugs, smirks, and looks away. I smile to myself.

She really is something.

"So, you really like this painting?" I ask.

"I do." She takes another sip of her gin and tonic as she looks up at the piece of art.

I grab a paper from the display.

"What are you doing?" She looks at me with a shocked stare. "You're not actually going to bid on anything are you?"

"It's a charity gala and I've got money to spare. Isn't that the point?" I scribble down a number.

Her mouth falls open. "That's twice what Marcus put!"

Dropping the paper into the box, I grin. "Oops."

"I can't believe you did that!"

"I guess the red side of my brain took over."

"How can you be so impulsive?"

"I'm guessing you don't make decisions without making an extensive pros and cons list first?"

She gives a quick laugh. "No… okay, maybe."

"Well, next time you see something that might be fun, don't think twice about it. Just do it."

She pauses as if considering the pros of cons of my statement.

I laugh. "You're already thinking too much!"

"You have very poor money management skills, you know."

"Seeing your reaction was well worth the price."

She smirks as she brings her drink to her lips.

"I like that you're honest," I say. "And smart."

She gives me a subtle smile. "Thank you, I work hard at both those things."

"But you're still hiding something."

She furrows her brow. "What?"

"You're a hockey fan."

"Well, sure. I saw the game the other day…"

"You've seen more than that. You knew Marcus Rock's name."

"*Everyone* knows Marcus Rock's name. He's the most famous defenseman on the Blades! There are billboards of his face all over the city."

"See? You know he's a defenseman."

She looks away. "Okay, maybe I'm a *bit* of a fan."

"I knew it!"

"I watch games every once in a while. So what?"

"Are you also a fan of mine?"

"We don't have to talk about that." She turns away and starts walking toward the next painting.

"Ooh, this is fun." I pursue her. "How long have you dreamed about meeting me?"

"I'm not doing this with you." She points at a painting of a river. "How about this one?"

"Oh no, I'm not letting you off that easy." I step into her line of sight.

But before I have a chance to bug her some more, I see someone approaching us.

"Look who decided to show up!" A deep, boisterous voice calls out. It can only be one person.

Turning around, I see that my suspicions are confirmed. Mike Balder waddles over to us, his round face red as usual. He sees Riley and his demeanor automatically changes. "And who is this young lady?"

"This is my girlfriend, Riley."

"Girlfriend? How lovely!" Balder's face softens.

Riley gives me a sharp look and I know she's mad that I'm already using the word 'girlfriend'. I give her a convincing look. *Just go with it.*

"Riley, this is the owner of the Seattle Blades, Mike Balder."

"Nice to meet you, Mr. Balder." She shakes his hand.

"So how long have you two been dating?" He asks.

We speak at the same time:

"One week—"

"One month—"

We exchange a look. *Crap.* We should have gone over our story first.

Riley smiles. "It's complicated."

"I see." Balder watches us suspiciously.

"Mr. Balder," Riley jumps in. "I've been a big fan of your team since the beginning. I think the Blades have a real shot of winning the cup this year."

Yes! So, she admits it. As if sensing my glee, she gives me a dangerous glance. I clear my throat.

Balder's ruddy face lights up. He turns to me. "You've got a good one here, Drake. She's definitely got the brains in this relationship."

"Blue brains," I say. I can't help but stifle a chuckle. She gives a quick smirk.

"So," Balder says. "How did you two meet?"

"Umm…" Riley looks at me for help.

"Riley interviewed me for the university paper."

"A sports columnist?" Balder raises an eyebrow.

"No," she says. "I'm in physio and biomechanics. I had questions about his routine so that I could collect data for a motor learning experiment I'm hoping to do."

I look at her, shocked that she came up with this story with such ease.

"Oh, I see," Balder says hesitantly. *Uh-oh,* I think. He looks suspicious. "What's your study?"

"Well… I'd like to use three-dimensional video and analog data to analyze an athlete's range of motion. By doing this, I hope to identify problem areas, especially areas that have been previously affected by an injury. Once those areas are identified, I can help provide solutions to healing those areas in the most optimal way using a mix of physiotherapy and biotechnology."

Balder's eyes widen and the suspicion disappears. "That's quite fascinating. You have the technology to do that?"

"Yes," she says. "I am currently taking a biomechanics and motor learning lab at Seattle University. We have the equipment at the school lab."

Impressed, I watch as she turns on the charm and loses the rigidity.

Balder is lost in his own thoughts for a moment. The jazz is still playing in the background as people chat and glasses clink.

"I like this," he says finally. "Once you finish your project, would you mind sending it to me?" Balder asks.

"Sure."

Balder digs into his wallet and pulls out a card. "My email address is there. I'd love to learn more about this."

"Of course, Mr. Balder." She takes his card.

"Please, call me Mike."

"Oh, you don't have to say that—"

"Yes, I do. The Blades aren't just an institution, we're a family. If you're Logan Drake's girlfriend, you're a part of our family, our team."

She shifts uncomfortably against me. "That's kind of you."

"Say, Drake. How'd you convince such a smart, capable woman to date you?"

"I don't know." I smile at her. "I guess I'm the red to her blue, complementary opposites."

"Well don't mess this up. She's got a good head on her shoulders."

"Thank you, Mr. Bal—I mean Mike." Riley gives me a smug smile.

"What's going on here?" A nasal voice says.

I lean into Riley and whisper, *"It's him. The journalist."*

The tall lanky man joins our circle.

"Logan." He nods. "Mr. Balder." He shakes Mr. Balder's hand. His eyes turn to Riley. "And this is?"

"Riley Jamieson." She puts out her hand. "Logan's girlfriend."

She says it with confidence. The sound of it feels good.

"Jake Turner of Seattle Sports Talk," the lanky man says.

"Pleasure." Riley shakes his hand.

"Ms. Jamieson is a med student at Seattle University," Mr. Balder says.

"Is that right?" Jake Turner raises his eyebrows rather unenthusiastically. He looks at me, unimpressed. "What happened, you bumped your head and end up in the ER?"

"Funny," I mumble.

"I'm not a med student," Riley corrects. "I'm a biomechanics student with a minor in sports injuries."

Jake turns away, clearly bored by this interaction.

"Great article the other day, Turner," I say. "Interesting insight into our team's power play dynamic."

He gives me a hesitant stare before getting distracted by our team captain, Rory Edgar. Rory is tall, has a short blond military buzzcut, and is beyond intimidating—almost like a drill sergeant ready to bark orders at anyone at any given time. It's no surprise, especially considering he was originally meant to join the marines before settling for hockey instead. He's impossible to miss. "Excuse me," Jake says.

And just like that, he's gone. I exhale.

"Damn."

Riley takes my hand and gives it a gentle squeeze. The small gesture is oddly reassuring.

"That man is so strange," Mr. Balder says. "I need to continue making my rounds but you kids have fun. Make sure to try the cannolis. The vanilla ones taste like heaven… just like my Nona Sophia used to make!"

"Will do."

"It was a pleasure meeting you," Riley says.

He pulls away.

"Oh!" Balder turns back. "Our next big event is the family skate in a few weeks. I look forward to seeing you there! And don't forget to email me!"

"Oh…" Riley shoots me a worried glance.

This could complicate things.

To my surprise, she looks at Balder and smiles. "I'll do my best to be there."

She will? That weird hopeful feeling rises up inside me again.

"Excellent! Don't forget your skates." Balder pulls away and is already greeting the next couple.

Once he's out of earshot, I turn to Riley.

"I've never seen him light up like that around me," I say. "Usually he's suspicious that I'm about to do something wrong."

"Well, he's got good reason…" She plays with the lip of her glass.

Ignoring her jab, I stare at Jake Turner who is scribbling in his notebook.

"I hope he's writing something good about me."

"I didn't realize you were such a sycophant," Riley says.

I raise my brows. "Syco-what?"

"Sycophant. Someone who gains attention by flattering powerful or influential people."

"So, a brown-noser?"

"You can put it that way."

I chuckle. "Yeah, that sounds like me. Anything for that Corazon trophy."

Staring at Balder, I see that he's asking one of the hockey wives to join him on the dancefloor. Jake Turner is standing near the dancefloor chatting with Coach Murphy.

"Would you like to dance?" I ask.

"What?"

"It's a thing people do when there's music and alcohol." I point to the dancefloor where several couples are dancing to smooth jazz.

"You're such a smart ass."

"Better than being a dumb ass." I smirk.

She rolls her eyes and looks out at the dance floor. "I'm not much of a dancer"

"Back and forth, side to side. It's easy. Come on." I take our glasses and set them down on a nearby table. "Follow me. It'll be fun."

She hesitates but her lips curl into a smile and I know I've got her. Taking her hand, I pull her onto the dance floor.

7

RILEY

Logan leads me to the dancefloor where we're surrounded by other couples.

Taking my hand in his, he slips his other hand around my waist. Our fingers interlace and he's pressing his palm against mine in an oddly intimate gesture. I look into his dark eyes. Adrenaline courses through my veins, tingling my fingertips.

We start moving to romantic jazz.

"Thank you," he says, "for doing all this." His breath smells good, minty.

"That's what I'm here for, right?"

I study him as we dance. His immaculately tailored blue suit still manages to show off his impressive biceps. His chiseled jaw is clean-shaven. He sure cleans up well. *Really well.* His dark eyes find me, clearly catching me staring. He smirks. My heart is pounding so hard I'm afraid he'll hear it. I look down.

"What?" He asks.

"Nothing."

"You're staring," he says in a low voice.

I clear my throat. "Why do you want to win the Corazon trophy so bad?"

I look back up into his stunning dark brown eyes.

"Because all the greatest hockey players that have ever lived have won that trophy—Namund, Alkin, Mazrik."

"So? You already know you're great at hockey. Why do you need a trophy?"

"It'll be proof that I'm great." He glances up at Jake Turner who's standing by the dance floor taking notes. "Sometimes I don't think I'll be happy until I have my name on that trophy."

"You're not happy now?"

He pauses. "I know I'll be happy when I get that trophy."

"So, simply playing hockey doesn't make you happy?"

"I never said that," he says defensively.

"You kind of just did."

He furrows his brow. "Well, hockey makes me happy because it helps me get what I want. You know, stats and glory."

I shake my head. "I can't believe that! You only like hockey because of the wins?"

"Yeah. How does that not make sense to you?"

"You can't treat something like a means to an end! You've got to treat it as an end in itself."

"Okay?" He raises his eyebrow. "And?"

"Life is more than just the gratification of winning. If you're always looking forward to the next win, you'll never enjoy anything. It won't be enough. You'll always have another to look forward to, and another. You need to enjoy every step of the way. That's the only way you'll ever live in life."

"And you enjoy every step of the way towards becoming a fancy doctor like your aunt?"

"Yes!"

"Oh right. You like studying. I forgot." There's a sarcastic tone in his voice. He pauses. "So are you enjoying this?"

"Criticizing your life's philosophy? Kind of, yes."

He laughs and I see a light shine in his eyes as they land on me. I smirk.

"I'm sorry for picking you apart," I say. "I just thought the amazing Logan Drake would love this game for what it is."

He watches me with a look of appreciation. His hand grips a bit tighter around my waist as we dance.

"I do," he says at last. "I guess I've been playing this game for so long that I forget why I got into it in the first place."

I smile. "I admit, I feel the same way sometimes at school. But you've got to enjoy every moment."

The music slows and we're barely even moving now. His body is tight against mine. My hand is around the back of his neck. There's nowhere else to look but into his eyes. Those dark, piercing eyes. *I could kiss him right now.*

I think about what he said earlier about how I need to take action without overthinking. But this is too dangerous a situation to stop thinking. I need to have my wits about me as he holds my waist, as he stands so close I can feel his minty breath on my lips.

"I hope you're as good a skater as you are a dancer." He smiles. "We could make a good team on the ice."

"Oh." I'm pulled out of my mini-trance. I'm reminded that this is all fake and that we only have a one-night contract. My head spins with confusion. "I just told Balder what he wanted to hear."

"Oh. I see." His enthusiasm deflates. He pulls his eyes from mine, looking around.

Did I embarrass him? Or worse—break his heart?

I follow his gaze and look around at the hulking hockey players dancing with their impeccably dressed partners.

"This was a one-night thing, right?" I ask. "That's what we said when we made the rules earlier."

"Oh, come on." His dark, dangerous eyes find me again. "Rules are meant to be broken."

The deep timbre of his voice lures me to another place for a moment.

"No, they're not," I say. "That's why they're rules!"

"Didn't you say you wanted to be more spontaneous?"

I lower my voice. "You really want me to be your fake girlfriend for more than one night?"

"Of course." Looking around to make sure nobody is within ear-shot, he lowers his voice to a deeper, more dangerous tone that excites something inside me. "Everybody already thinks we're dating. It'd be perfect."

"How long would you want to do this for?" I ask.

"How about until the end of the season? We'll only have to meet up for about six events over the course of four months."

That wouldn't be too bad.

"And we'll keep it boring. No drama." His dark eyes hold mine. "What do you think? This is your chance to be more impulsive."

Pulling away from his magnetic eyes, I look around at all the fancy people chatting and dancing around me.

"What are you going to give me in exchange?"

"I'll pay off your student debt, your dorm fees, your meal cards…"

My jaw falls open but I compose myself quickly. Having read about his multimillion-dollar trade deal with the Blades, I decide to push him a bit. "That's it?"

"And I'll give you extra money for whatever you want—books, clothes—"

"—lab equipment?"

"Sure."

I straighten my posture and smile to myself. "Okay."

He raises his eyebrows. "Okay? Okay as in… you want to do this?"

"Yes. You need your image cleaned up and I need the money. And like you said, everyone already thinks we're dating."

"I thought you didn't date." He smirks as if he's just outwitted me.

"This isn't really dating," I say. "If I only have to see you twice a month, and we know we can keep the whole money thing a secret, then the benefits outweigh the risks."

He sighs. "And just when I thought you were starting to like me for me."

Another couple bumps into us. They apologize quickly before spinning away.

"Come." I pull Logan off the dancefloor and across the gallery.

"Where are we going?"

"We're getting your car from valet so you can drive me home and we can have somewhere private to talk about this."

"Drive you home? But the night's just begun."

I pull my phone out of my clutch. "It's half past eleven."

"Really? Whoa. Time flies when you're having fun."

I look at him, trying to figure out if he's trying to be cute.

"Come on." We make our way to the entrance where we get our coats from the coat check. Logan hands his ticket to the heavily tattooed valet attendant. When the attendant disappears, Logan turns to me.

"So what do we need to talk about?"

"If we do this, we need rules."

We make our way outside where the rain has finally eased up.

"More rules?" He raises his eyebrows.

"A contract." Opening my glittery clutch, I pull out a folded piece of paper and a pen. "We have to make sure there's a line so we don't cross it."

"You carry pens and paper around with you?"

"They're study notes." I show him the opposite side of the page which covered in tiny biochemistry notes. "I study them whenever I have free time."

"I don't know what else I expected." He watches me as I write our initials at the top: RJ + LD. "I'm sure you know exactly what the rules will be."

"Rule number one," I say as I scribble everything onto the piece of paper. "This only lasts until the end of the season, when the awards are given out."

"Agreed."

The black luxury car drives up to the door and the attendant hops out, pulling Logan and me out of our conversation. The attendant hands Logan the keys while Logan hands back a one-hundred-dollar bill.

"Did you just—" I stare in shock as the attendant pockets the bill. "You know what, never mind. Come on."

We climb into the car as Logan fires up the car and starts driving.

"So," Logan says. "I'm guessing there's a second rule?"

I clear my throat and start writing again. "Rule two: everything we do must be in public, especially any PDA."

"PDA?"

"Public displays of affection. You know, any hand-holding, dancing, kissing." Looking up, I see he's smiling.

"I know," he says smugly. "I just wanted to hear you explain it."

I roll my eyes. "You're super annoying, you know that, right?"

"Is there a rule three?"

"Rule three." I swallow. "No falling in love."

"Was that a possibility for you?" He takes his eyes off the road to give me a self-assured smirk.

"Of course not! You and I would never work for a whole number of reasons."

"Why do you need rule three then if you don't think it'll ever happen?"

"Because I don't trust you," I say bluntly.

"Me?" He acts surprised.

"Yeah, you *clearly* like me."

He laughs. "You're direct, I like that."

"Don't start with that." I hold up the contract. "It's number three in the contract."

He holds up a hand. "I'm not doing anything! Besides, liking you is not the same as loving you."

"It's a slippery slope. Besides, you're flirting with me. That breaks rule number two too."

"It's part of my personality. And it seems hypocritical of you to accuse me of this when you like me *way* more than I like you."

"What? No, I don't! If anything, you like me. I've seen the way you look at me!"

He casts a glance in my direction as he pulls onto the highway. "How do I look at you?"

"Like you're looking at me right now."

He's smirking. "The lady doth protest too much."

"Now you're quoting Shakespeare? Who *are* you?"

"That's from Shakespeare? I thought it was from The Simpsons."

"Of course you did. Oh boy" I laugh as I rub my face. "What the hell did I get myself into?"

Pulling off the highway, he pulls onto campus and parks next to the library.

I hand him the pen. "Shall we make this official?"

"In a hurry to be my fake girlfriend, aren't we?"

"You know, I'm suddenly having second thoughts." I make a gesture as if I'm about to rip up the contract.

"Okay, I'm sorry! I'll stop with the teasing."

Casting a sharp gaze in his direction, I hand him the contract. My eyes linger as he signs his name.

I'm getting Logan Drake's signature.

The hockey fan in me is freaking out while the feminist in me is dying a little. I try to remember what Jane told me back in the dorms: this is acting, this is theater. None of it is real.

Logan hands me the pen. I stare at the blank space next to his name. This is it. This is my chance to be spontaneous. Adrenaline rushes through me as I sign my name.

"I guess it's official," he says.

"I guess so."

We sit in the car in silence.

I fold the contract and put it carefully in my clutch. I place my hand on the door handle. "I guess I'll see you at the skating event."

"I'll send you the details."

"Great." Unsure what the protocol is for saying goodbye to a fake boyfriend, I give him a tight-lipped smile as I open my door. "See you around."

"Riley?"

"Yes?" I look back at him.

"Thanks for a fun night." He smiles and this time it's genuine, momentarily taking my breath away. I catch myself smiling back.

I can resist him.

I can resist that infectious laugh, his seductive words, the charm in his gaze. *Right?* I remind myself this is about business. Even though he's hot as hell and I can't stop staring into his mesmerizing eyes, I can't let my feelings—or my libido—get involved. This is purely business.

"Good night, Logan."

Trying to keep it cool, I get out of the car and rush back to my dorm as quickly as I can.

What the eff did I get myself into?

8

RILEY

That week, March arrives with warm and foggy weather which is perfect for spending time in the library. Tucked away in the corner at my favorite desk, I work on my proposal for my biomechanics project.

As I attempt to work, my mind drifts to Logan and how easy conversation flowed between us. I think about how he looked at me when we danced, the way he held my hand.

God, he was so handsome it's hard not being completely entranced by him. Now I understand why he gets so much attention from women, the media, online… basically everywhere!

What was I thinking?

Money. That's what I was thinking. A giant boatload of money that I can dive into and swim around in.

Okay, not really. But it'll be enough to pay off all my bills and then some. With that kind of freedom, I can spend all my extra time getting lab experience.

When I make my way back to my room to prepare for that afternoon's Advanced Physics Lab, I see Jane sitting on her bed. She's wearing a pink sports bra and black bicycle shorts while she works on her laptop. Her dark hair is in a giant messy bun. She looks up at me with her blue eyes and a knowing smirk.

"What?" I ask.

She turns her laptop around to show me a photo of Logan and me at the gala.

Oh *god*. I'm on the internet.

"You went on a date with Logan Drake?" She asks. "And you didn't tell me?"

My first challenge.

I nod. "He asked me to go to a charity gala with him."

It feels weird calling it a date, but with the fancy clothes, the cocktails, the dancing (not to mention the bubbling sexual chemistry), it definitely felt like one.

"Oh my *god*, this is huge! Lucky bitch!"

I furrow my brow. "Hey!"

She tosses her work aside and focuses all her attention on me. "Tell me everything!"

"Well, there's not much to tell." I shrug. "We talked, we looked at art, we danced."

"What's he like?"

I pause as I stare at the photo of us. I remember how good he smelled. I remember the way he smiled when he teased me.

"He was funny. And charming."

Jane squeals. "You're blushing!"

"No, I'm not!"

"Oh, sure. Whatever." Jane rolls her eyes and smiles mischievously. "Are you seeing him again?"

I nod.

"Yay! This is so freaking exciting! My girl is finally getting it."

Not really, I think to myself. Unless 'it' means money.

There's a knock at the door. We exchange a look.

"Were you expecting anyone?" I ask.

She shakes her head. Opening the door, I see an unwelcome face.

"Heyyy beautiful," Keith appears in the doorway looking just as disheveled as usual. Jane and I groan in unison.

"What do you want, Keith?" I ask.

"I want you, baby."

"Please leave." I close the door but he stops me.

"Don't worry, honey, I'm not here for you." He looks at Jane who's still sitting on her bed. "I'm actually here to ask Jane something."

I open the door wider so she can see.

"What?" Jane asks in a bored voice.

"Do you want to work together for the Investigative Journalism final?"

"No! Not after you bailed on your group project and then cheated in Mr. Ross' class last year."

"Fine," Keith says grumpily. "Don't tell anyone about that, by the way. I can still get kicked out of school for that."

"Can you leave now?" Jane asks.

Keith ignores her and looks back at me. "Wanna go out tonight? Happy hour at Merryman's is at 7."

"She has a boyfriend," Jane says.

Keith's eyes widen. "Is that true?"

Realizing that Jane is technically right, I nod. "Oh yeah. I *do* have a boyfriend."

"What's his name?" He asks suspiciously.

"Logan." There's confidence in my voice.

"Oh." He frowns, realizing that I answered too quick to be lying. "Well, shit." Without any further hesitation, he walks off.

"What a loser," Jane says. "Everyone knows Tony's is the better campus bar."

"I'll have to take your word for it." Making sure he's gone, I close the door. "Why haven't I ever lied about having a boyfriend before? I feel like a weight's been lifted off my shoulders."

"Well… you're not lying now," Jane says as she grabs her laptop and starts tapping away.

"Oh. Right."

Get your shit together, Riley.

There's another knock at the door. My smile disappears. "Please don't tell me that's Keith again."

Ready to throw a whole mess of expletives at him, I open the door but I quickly bite my tongue when I see a mail carrier instead.

"Riley Jamieson?" She asks.

"Yes?"

"This is for you." She hands me a brown envelope with the university's logo stamped onto it. I've seen enough envelopes like it to know it's a tuition statement.

"Thank you," I say miserably.

"And this." She pulls a large square package into view. I instantly know what it is.

She helps me slide it into the apartment and leaves.

"What is *that?*" Jane sits up with hungry eyes. "A present?"

I pull the covering off to reveal the red and blue painting that Logan bid on at the art gallery the other night.

"A painting," I say, smiling to myself. "From the gala last night."

"Look, there's a note." Jane grabs the card but I pull it out of her hand before she reads anything. My eyes scan the text for anything that can give me away before I read it out loud.

Riley,

Since you liked this so much, I figured you should have it.

Your Boyfriend,

Logan

"Oh my god!" Jane is reading over my shoulder. "Boyfriend? He is *so* cute."

"Yeah, *too* cute," I mumble to myself, noting that he's breaking rule number two in our contract.

Once Jane exhausts all her gushing and excitement, she grabs the painting and holds it up to the wall.

"Where shall we put it? I'm thinking over here where the light hits it." She takes down a framed poster of Casablanca and puts the painting up instead.

While Jane is busy making sure the painting is level, I open the tuition statement and quickly scan it, stopping abruptly when I notice the balance at the bottom. Half the tuition has already been paid off.

Holy shit!

"Dating Logan Drake sure has its perks," Jane says as she admires the newly mounted painting.

"It sure does," I mumble to myself as I stare at the statement a little while longer. Eventually, I fold the statement and slip it away in my desk with the rest of them.

Jane spins around. "This guy must really like you."

I look up at the painting and smile.

"Yeah," I say. "I guess he does."

Maybe being Logan Drake's fake girlfriend wouldn't be so bad after all.

9

LOGAN

"Five paintings—five!" Marcus cradles his head in his hands.

We're sitting on the bus with the rest of the team, traveling from our San Francisco hotel to the arena for tonight's game against the Whips.

"I have the money to buy them," Marcus continues, "but I didn't think I'd actually win them."

"That's what happens when you bid on everything," I say.

"I don't even have enough wall space in my apartment for that many paintings!"

"You can sell them, can't you?"

He looks at me. "Do you want one?"

"No dice, buddy. I already bought one."

"Do you even have room for a painting? I thought your walls were reserved for trophies."

"I have space for the Corazon." Looking down at my phone, I scroll through the sports headlines looking for my name.

"Dude, you're obsessed."

"Maybe. But don't worry, I'm still focusing on the cup too. First, we win the cup, then I win the trophy."

Marcus gives me a semi-toothy smile, having just lost one in our previous game. "I like that plan."

"Look." I show him the headline of an article in this week's paper: *Gala Shows Charitable Side of Seattle Blades.*

"Read it," he says.

"On Saturday, the Blades Organization hosted a charity fundraiser for the new children's hospital, showing off a more community-oriented side to the team. Politicians, doctors, athletes, and local celebrities rubbed elbows and drank cocktails while raising money for the cause."

I skip the boring parts.

"A number of celebrities and players bid—and went home—with prizes, including Logan Drake, who also brought in an additional 1.2 million for a stick he donated for the night's occasion."

"Good job, buddy." Marcus nudges me with his massive elbow.

"Spinner told me to donate that stick. Best idea he's ever had." I keep reading. "*But is this genuine? Or is this a blatant attempt to adjust perceptions of his notorious behavior? Everyone knows about his shameful fight on the ice with Harrison Cooper and the cheating scandal not long before that.* Which was fake," I add. "*But now there are rumors that his injuries are affecting his game on the ice*—Okay, that's enough of that."

I swipe away the story.

"Gee, that guy really has it in for you," Marcus says.

"Yeah, I don't know what his problem is. But look." I hold the phone out so Marcus can see the picture of Riley and me chatting by a painting. She's smiling, looking just as beautiful as I remember. "We look good together, don't we?"

"I like her," Marcus says. He pauses, waiting for me to say something. "Do you?"

"Of course. She's smart, beautiful, funny…"

"You seem smitten." Marcus smiles cheekily.

"I seem what?"

"In *love.*"

"No, no. Well, maybe. I don't know." As I'm scrolling through the article, something catches my attention. "Holy shit, listen to this: *Harrison Cooper raked in six points in the other night's 5-2 win over the Atlantic Aces. The Cleveland Crusher's six points consisted of three goals—one of them a shorthanded breakaway. This is Cooper's third hat-trick this season. And this isn't the first time he's racked up more than five points in regulation this month, either. 'With this kind of playing, he's looking at all sorts of records and trophies in his future,' Coach Brauer said after the game.*"

"Wow." Marcus raises his brow. "He's incredible."

"Which means we have to be better." I swipe the app away and put my phone down. "We're tied for points right now. I have to do better than him."

"Better than six points in one night?"

"We can do that. Three goals, three assists. I'll feed the puck to you, you feed it to me. Easy-peasy."

Marcus laughs. "Right. Easy. Why don't we just win every game, every night?"

"Focus on the goal and you can't miss."

"Hey." Marcus nods toward my phone. "Don't pay too much attention to all that news stuff. And don't worry about Coop either. You guys are both good players in different ways."

"If I don't pay attention to hockey, what else am I supposed to pay attention to?" I ask.

Riley flashes through my mind and I shake her away. If I start thinking about her, I won't be able to stop.

Marcus shrugs. "I'm listening to a really cool podcast right now about bees."

"Bees? Like… the birds and the bees?"

Marcus smiles innocently. "Yeah, I guess they talk about birds too sometimes."

"That's not what I meant... you know what? Never mind." Before I have a chance to bring up hockey again, I'm distracted by a notification for an incoming text. It's from Riley.

RILEY: Thank you for the painting.

I smile. Just as I'm about to compose a text, another one from her pops up.

RILEY: But gifts are unnecessary.

I type back and send her a response.

LOGAN: For a second there I thought the ice queen melted away.

As I wait for a response, I stare at the screen obsessively. I finally force myself to look out the window at all the boats on the ocean. My phone buzzes in my hand.

RILEY: I thought hockey players liked ice.

I smile. Not knowing what else to send, I put the first thing that comes to mind.

LOGAN: :)

There's no response. I'm sure she's carefully crafting a long paragraph about how I'm breaking rule two, or three, or whatever. I type back in an attempt to cut her off before I receive a scolding.

LOGAN: will you watch me play tonight?

I wait for a response that doesn't come. The bus comes to an abrupt halt.

"We're here." Marcus wraps his headphones around his phone. Everyone gets out of their seats and files off the bus. I check my phone a few more times but there are no new messages.

No, I can't do this.

The last time I got involved with a woman, it ended poorly for me. It's better if I focus on hockey. *Just* hockey.

"Before today's practice, we have some things to address." Coach Murphy looks at us once we're all in the locker room. "First thing's first, Barkley's back with us after a two-week absence. Good to have you back, Barkley."

"Way to go, Gopher. We're proud of you for recovering from such a traumatic injury," Rock says.

The rest of the team laughs. Normally players recover from injuries sustained on the ice, but Barkley strained his lower back picking up his kid's toy gopher, earning him his new nickname.

"Glad to be back, Coach."

"Prove all these clowns wrong today, won't ya, Barkley?"

"Yes, Coach."

Coach clears his throat. "Now to the important stuff. Two playoff spots have already been taken and it's a tight race for the rest of them. The Whips are on a five-game winning streak and if they win, they pull way ahead of us in the standings. We need to win this one to keep our playoff dreams alive. Let's end their streak and start our own."

"Yeah!"

"Let's get 'em!"

"Come on, guys," Coach says. "Let's play some hockey!"

During the game, the outside world melts away. Nothing exists but the ice, the teams, and the puck. The energy in the arena is electric as the guys are amped up and ready to play. We have a rocky first period where two dumb plays put us down 2-0. But in the second period, I manage to set Marcus up twice, allowing him to score. Along with a shorthanded goal by Gopher, we go into the third period with a one-goal lead. I manage to score a goal in the third while Edgar scores an empty-net goal to put us up 6-3 as the final score.

Although I managed a goal and two assists, I knew I could have done better and I should have. After showering, I rush to my locker and check my phone. Cleveland played tonight. If Coop played as good as he did the other day, then I'm screwed. I check the stats of the game to see if Coop score any goals or assists. As I'm navigating my sports app, a text message from Riley pops up.

RILEY: Good job tonight, Mr. Drake

Something about seeing her name on my screen makes my heart beat faster. I smile to myself.

LOGAN: Why thank you, Ms. Jamieson

I try to think of something witty to say in relation to her watching me all night but I can't think fast enough. She texts me first.

RILEY: I've been thinking about it and I think we should go on a date.

I stare at my screen.

Am I reading this right?

I read the text a few times, trying to process what I'm seeing.

LOGAN: You want to go on a date… with me? Are you sure? I think this counts as some sort of rule-breaking.

The three dots appear and disappear several times. I envision her texting furiously, writing a dissertation on why we should go on a date. The thought of it makes me chuckle to myself.

RILEY: We need to get to know each other better. We already messed up when telling Balder about our dating history. It'll be easier if we actually knew a bit about each other.

LOGAN: Oh, those are the reasons? I thought it was because you liked me.

RILEY: Nope.

That response comes so quickly that I can't help but feel a bit hurt.

RILEY: I'm free Wednesday. I know you don't have a game that night.

LOGAN: You know my schedule already? Such an attentive girlfriend.

I add that last part, knowing it'll get under her skin.

RILEY: See you then

LOGAN: :)

She doesn't respond. Smiling to myself and feeling accomplished, I put my phone into my bag, completely forgetting to search for Coop's stats. Grabbing my stuff, I run out to catch a ride with the guys back to the hotel.

10

LOGAN

As I navigate my way to Riley's building so that we can go on our date, my head fills with thoughts wondering what her life is like.

What does she do for fun? Does she have lots of friends? Does she have a secret boyfriend that she hasn't told me about?

Making my way down the gray hallway of her dorm building, I knock on her door. It opens and there she is. Riley's blond hair is in a wild messy bun on top of her head and she's wearing big round glasses, sweat pants, and a plain white t-shirt (knotted at the waist) showing way more skin than I was expecting from her. I keep my gaze at eye-level.

"Logan!" She pushes her glasses up her nose. "What are you doing here? I told you I was going to be thirty minutes late."

"I know. But I was already in the neighborhood when you texted me so I figured it couldn't hurt to swing by and hang around until you're read. I figured you're late because you have homework to do?"

She nods. "How'd you know?"

I smirk. "A wild guess."

She eyes the brown paper bag in my hand. "What's that?"

I hold up the bag which smells like apples and cinnamon. "I figured you're probably hungry from studying so hard."

Her eyes grow wide. "Oh my god, is that a Jarry's apple strudel?"

"The one and only."

"Oh my god, my savior!" She grabs the bag out of my hand, opens it, and takes a big whiff. Her eyes practically roll back in her head.

"You're welcome."

"Come in," she says as she pulls the strudel out of the bag and takes a bite. "I was just finishing up. Just a few more things and I'll get ready."

I step into her room. There are two beds, one on each side. In between, there's a desk and a mobile rack of clothing. The desk is covered with books, notebooks, and pens.

"This place is the same size as my kitchen," I say as I look around.

"Wow, great humble-brag."

I chuckle. "Sorry. I just didn't realize you lived in such a cramped place! It's just like the kinds of places you see in the movies and on TV."

"That's dorm life for you." She takes another bite of the strudel and moans. *"Doyouwhatsom?"*

She holds up what's left.

I wave her off. "It's all yours."

She licks her lips. "This probably doesn't fit into your super strict diet, huh?"

"Not really, no. But I'll live vicariously and watch you eat it." I smile as I watch her.

"Yeah, because that's not creepy at all."

I smirk and look around the room. Even though it's small, Riley and her roommate have made it very homey. There are twinkle lights around the ceiling and all sorts of pictures and motivational quotes on the wall. I notice that the red and blue painting I bought for her is hanging over one of the beds.

"Nice art," I say.

Riley looks up and smiles. "Thanks, a friend gave it to me."

"So you *do* consider me your friend."

"Yeah. And, you know, a fake date too."

I chuckle. "Right."

Continuing to look around the room, I look at the rack of clothes. A familiar black, silver and blue garment catches my eye. "Hello, what's this?"

I get up to investigate further. The colors are unmistakable. It's a Seattle Blades jersey.

"Oh shit." She sets the strudel aside and pounces onto my back just as I grab the jersey from the rack. "Give that to me!"

She reaches for the jersey as her legs wrap around me so that I'm holding her piggy-back-style as we engage in a tug-of-war for the garment, but it's too late. My suspicions have been confirmed.

"Is that—my name and number?" I manage to turn the jersey around and see 'Drake 13'. "It is!"

"No!" She's still struggling with me.

"Oh, this is *good.* Riley Jamieson bought my jersey." A sense of pride blooms inside my chest. I look back at her guilty, dejected face.

Her body goes limp as she slumps against me, giving up the fight. "I only bought it so I could look more like your girlfriend."

"Really? Because this jersey was a limited-edition version from when I first joined the team."

"Ugh." She slides off my back in defeat. "Fine. You got me."

I turn to face her. Her face is bright red.

"You're an even bigger fan of hockey than I thought. And an even bigger fan of mine." I smirk.

"Yes. I'll admit it. I like hockey, okay? And I like the Blades. You already knew that."

I smirk. "And you like me."

"Oh *god*, your ego is going to be huge now. Even bigger than I thought it could be." She rubs her face. "Look, I don't want you to think I was some sort of sports groupie or anything."

"I never said you were." This is too good. I can't stop smiling. "If you own this, does that mean I'm your favorite player?"

She crosses her arms and tilts her head to the side as she looks at me. "Well, you've had some issues over the past few months. And your penalty kill is atrocious."

"Okay, okay. You don't have to rip my soul apart right after giving me such a beautiful gift." I hold the jersey to my chest.

She smiles. "You're not all bad though. I mean, it's true that I almost had to drop you from my fantasy team."

"Fantasy team?" The smile creeps onto my face again. "You surprise me more every day, Ms. Jamieson." I watch her for a moment, tempted to pull her in and kiss her. I have to mentally remind myself that she's a fake girlfriend, not a real one.

She snatches the jersey out of my hands. As she's about to put it back on the hanger, I stop her.

"Will you—"

She turns to face me. "Will I what?"

"Will you put it on for me?"

She rolls her eyes. "Oh lord, I wish you had never seen this."

"But I did." I reach over and grab her waist, pulling her close. "Tell me more about how you put me on your fantasy team."

She puts her hands on my chest and looks up at me with those big gray eyes. Her lips part and close again. For a fleeting moment, I feel like she's going to kiss me. Instead, her brow furrows.

"What are you doing here?" She pushes me off her. "Our date is not for another fifteen minutes."

"If you don't want me to come by anymore, I won't."

She bites her lower lip.

"No," she says. "It's alright. I don't mind you coming over. As long as you bring more strudel with you." She smirks as she looks at me, then quickly looks away. "Just give me some warning next time. I'll put real clothes on."

"But I like you like this. It's Riley in her natural habitat wearing the traditional outfit of her people—sweat pants."

She gives me a dangerous look.

"Kidding." I put my hands up defensively. "I'll give you a warning next time. Even though I would *love* to catch you wearing this jersey one day. Are you sure you don't want to put it on right now?"

"Yes, I'm very sure." She pulls away. "Let me finish eating and I'll get ready for our fake date."

Resting her elbows on the desk, she bends over, sticking her butt out as she eats the rest of the strudel. As she takes a bite, she looks over at me.

"Are you sure you don't want any?"

I smirk as I watch her. "I guess having one bite can't hurt."

11

RILEY

A few minutes later I kick Logan out of my room as I get ready for our "get to know each other" date.

Date.

It feels way too much like a date. A *real* one.

Wearing jeans, a loose black top, and blue shoes, I take my hair out of its messy bun, letting it cascade down into perfect waves. I wasn't originally going to put too much effort into my appearance but after seeing how handsome Logan was in his black t-shirt, fitted jeans, and brown dress shoes, I decide to upgrade my look. I even try a few makeup tricks Jane taught me. I keep my glasses on, which accentuate my eyes.

My cheeks flush hot as I hang my Blades jersey back on the rack. I should have hidden it but how was I supposed to know Logan Drake would be in my room?

God, I wanted to kiss him so badly. It took every bit of restraint I had not to. *Even though I wanted to.*

I shake the thoughts away as I stuff my clutch into my purse and leave my room, rounding the corner to see Logan waiting at the building's entrance. He smiles when he sees me.

"You look beautiful," he says. He puts his hands up. "I know, I know, rule number two."

"It's okay," I say. "We're in public."

He smiles. "Ready?"

I nod. He takes my hand in his, interlacing our fingers. A thrill rushes through my body. For a moment I feel like it's too much, like I can't do this.

"So, where are we going?" He asks as we start walking through the campus courtyard.

"The campus bar, Tony's."

"You go there a lot?"

I shake my head. "Not really. My roommate does."

"When's the last time you had a boyfriend?" He asks.

"Whoa! You can't just ask that."

"Why not? I thought we were supposed to get to know each other." He looks at me innocently.

"Yeah, but you don't start with such intense questions!"

"What kind of questions do we start with then?"

"Let's see." I thought up a bunch of questions yesterday but now they've all slipped from my mind. It's hard to think when Logan Drake is staring at me with that sexy, smoldering stare. "Okay, do you have a nickname?"

He shakes his head. "It's just Logan. Or Drake when I'm on the ice. But my mom calls me Logi-bear."

"Aww." I stifle a laugh. "Cute."

As we walk, I notice students staring at Logan. Some of them are pulling their phones out to take photos.

"This must happen a lot," I say.

"Oh, you have no idea."

We make our way into the student bar. There are about six other people at the cramped bar already but we manage to find an empty booth where we sit opposite each other. Rihanna is playing on the jukebox. All eyes seem to be on him while his are on me.

"You look great." His gaze holds me in place.

"You said that already."

"Because it's true."

I study the menu, trying to hide my smile. I still can't believe Logan Drake is my fake boyfriend.

"You're shaking," he says.

"No, I'm not." I put the menu down.

"Do you want a beer?" Logan signals for the waitress who has been standing by the bar, watching him like a hawk since we arrived. She scurries to our table a bit too eagerly.

"Hi Mr. Drake," she says with an overaffected voice. She completely ignores me as she squeezes her arms together, accentuating her cleavage.

Oh geez, seriously? I hope I don't look or sound that desperate when I talk to him.

"Can I get a pint of your best beer?" He smiles at her.

"Of course." The way she's staring at him, she may as well have hearts for eyes.

"And Riley?" He asks, looking at me.

"I'll have a pint of the same thing."

The waitress finally looks at me, her smile fading as if she's finally realizing Logan is not alone.

"Coming right up."

She stumbles as she backs away, smiling at him the whole time.

"Do you usually have this effect on women?" I ask as I look back at him.

"Only if they're human." He smirks. "And not named Riley."

I laugh. "That wouldn't be the first time a guy thinks I'm cold."

"I can't say I'm surprised." He taps the table with his fingers. "So, you like beer?"

"Sometimes."

"How many do you usually drink on a night off?"

"One pint is usually enough. Actually, I'm a half-pinter."

"Me too." He laughs. "We can't really drink that much when we play every second day."

"Gotta keep the temple clean?"

"That's right." He smirks.

The waitress comes by with our drinks faster than I thought possible. She has a lot more cleavage on display this time around than she did before.

"Can I get you anything else?" She asks.

"That's all for now," he says.

"Alright, well let me know!"

"Will do." He barely looks at her.

She pouts before making her way back to the bar, looking back over her shoulder to see if he's watching. He's not.

He's looking at me.

I suppress a smile.

"Wow," I say. "You get first-class service."

"I'm used to it. One of the perks of being famous, I guess." He takes a sip of his beer.

"You know that waitress has been salivating over you since we walked in."

"I know. That's why I'm trying not to make eye contact."

"Pretty girls with nice boobs aren't your thing?"

He smirks. "Not when I already have a girlfriend."

He reaches over the table and takes my hand, lightly moving his thumb over mine. It's an intimate gesture that, for a fleeting moment, makes me feel like this is real.

The waitress clearly looks miffed. I can't help but feel a bit flattered. I've never been the object of envy before, especially not from a woman who looks like she can get any guy she wants.

This fake girlfriend thing is fun.

"So." He narrows his dark eyes. "Let's get to know each other."

My finger flinches against his. "Okay. Why did you become a hockey player?"

"Because I'm good at it."

"Oh, come on. There's got to be something more than that."

"I've always been very skilled on my feet. And with my hands." His finger presses against mine, sending a jolt to my core. I instinctively pull away, composing myself so that he doesn't realize how frazzled I am.

"What's your favorite food?" I ask, changing the subject from how adept his hands are.

"Lasagna," he says without hesitation. "Gotta get those pre-game carbs in. Yours?"

I think for a minute. "Granola bars."

He laughs. "Seriously? Granola bars?"

"What's wrong with a granola bar? It's got fiber, carbs, protein. It's calorie-dense so I don't have to take long breaks for lunch."

"Even your meals are efficient. You really are a robot, aren't you?"

I let out a sharp laugh. "A robot? Come on, you don't drink protein shakes or granola bars or anything?"

"Well, I do. But I have taste-buds and I'm also not a psychopath who doesn't enjoy food."

"I like food! I liked the apple strudel, didn't I?"

"But it's not your favorite."

"Well, it's not practical or efficient. Plus, my breath still smells like cinnamon, so thanks for that."

He chuckles. "It smells fine to me. Besides, I had a bite of it so we're both cinnamon-y together."

I suppress a smile. "Well, maybe once I'm not a student anymore, I'll change my eating habits. It's hard not to have home-cooked meals without a kitchen."

"You ever heard of a thing called a restaurant?"

I laugh. "If I had the money for that, I wouldn't be here with you."

He straightens in his seat. "I guess that's true. At least you don't have to worry about food anymore with all the money you have now. The thought of you living off dry granola bars depresses me."

"Yeah," I say absently. The truth of why we're here dawns on me. I reclaim my hand from the table and place it in my lap. He stares at me for a moment.

"Favorite ice cream flavor?"

I laugh. "Is this really what it means to get to know each other?"

"It's the little things that are important, right?"

"I guess that's true. Hmm, I'd say my favorite flavor is vanilla."

He makes a face. "Vanilla? That's so boring!"

"Are you really going to criticize every single answer of mine?"

He laughs. "I'm sorry, I didn't mean to. It's just…vanilla? Why?"

"It's classic and delicious. Besides, you can mix it with anything. Chocolate, fruit, sprinkles, butterscotch, mint… the list goes on. You can keep it simple or make it crazy and wild. It's versatile. What?" I notice he's staring at me with a lazy smile.

"I'm just thinking about you being crazy and wild."

"Logan!"

He laughs. "Sorry! You said it and my mind went somewhere."

Laughing faintly, I look down.

Now *my* mind is somewhere. My cheeks are getting hot and I know he for sure can see them turning pink

"Excuse me," I say before pulling out of the booth and heading to the ladies' room. I draw a few envious stares on my way there.

Finally gaining some privacy in the bathroom, I splash some cool water on my cheeks and wrists before staring at myself in the mirror. I look flushed, but happy. There's a sparkle in my eye.

Straightening out my outfit and fluffing my hair a bit, I make my way back to the table. When I see our booth, I pause. There's someone sitting in my spot across from Logan.

As I get closer, I realize it's Keith. He's fangirling over Logan.

"Hey," I say, standing by the table.

Keith looks up at me. "Riley! Look who's having a beer here at *our* university! Wait... whoa, you look smoking hot. Did someone say bonertown?"

I roll my eyes.

"Show the lady some respect." Logan clenches his jaw, giving Keith the hardest death glare I've ever seen.

"Oh. Sorry."

"Keith, get out of my spot."

His eyes grow wide. "*You're* Logan's date?"

"I'm her boyfriend," he says. "And if you don't show Riley respect, you're going to have to deal with me."

I give Keith a smug smile as he stares at me suspiciously.

"Oh…of—of course," Keith stutters. "Wait—can I borrow some change for the jukebox? I desperately want to listen to some Bieber. I've had that one stupid song stuck in my head all day." He puts his hand on my purse, which is on the seat next to him.

"Fucking seriously, dude?" Logan is now livid.

"I forgot mine back at res. It's just a few quarters." He looks back at me. "I'll pay you back."

"Fine." I look at Logan, who's still seething while staring at Keith. I tap my foot against Logan's. He looks at me. *"It's fine,"* I mouth.

Keith has his back to us as he searches my purse in the corner of the booth.

"*Today,* please," I say.

"Okay, okay. It's just your zipper is stuck—just a few more moments—okay, there." He turns around, one hand holding coins, while the other is holding his cracked phone.

He shuffles out of the booth seat. "It was nice meeting ya. Big fan."

"Right." Logan glares.

When Keith's gone, I slide into the booth.

"Sorry about that," I say.

"Don't apologize for him. Why'd you give him money anyway?"

I shrug. "It was just a few quarters. And I see him every day. It's easier to just be nice to him otherwise everything he says is pure vitriol."

"You're too nice for that ass."

"I know." I take a sip of my beer.

"Does he act like that toward you a lot?"

"All the freaking time," I say. "At least ever since we slept together."

Logan raises his eyebrows in shock. "You slept with *him?*"

I let out a short laugh. "Mr. Drake, are you jealous?"

"You said no to a date with me, but you had sex with *that* guy?"

I lean over and touch his clean-shaven cheek. "Oh, my poor baby. Was I your first time ever getting rejected? Is your ego hurt?"

He puts his hand on his chest. "A little bit, yes! Seriously though…*him?*"

Sitting back in my seat, enjoying this breakdown of Logan Drake's ego, I smirk as I take another sip of beer.

"Let's get back to our questions, shall we?" I put the beer down. "What's your go-to breakfast?"

"We're onto the food again, are we?"

"You started it! Besides, when I'm not getting laid I focus on food."

He raises an eyebrow as he leans in. "How long has it been since you've gotten laid?"

I raise my chin and look away. "You don't need to know that."

"It's been a while, huh?" He leans back. That devilish smirk on his lips appears on his lips, coaxing me to tell him all my secrets. It's going to be my undoing.

"What? No." I pause. "Well, it's been six months."

"So, it *has* been a while."

"Not really. If it's always as bad as it is with Keith, it can wait."

This catches his attention and he leans in again. "It wasn't good?"

"Sex is…overrated," I say. Wow. I can't believe that just came out of my mouth. I look at my beer—which is almost empty. No wonder.

Logan lowers his voice. "You know, if that's truly what you believe then I think you've been doing it wrong."

"You don't know my sex life."

He laughs. "Anyone who says sex is overrated isn't doing it right. Maybe the way you're doing it is a bit too…vanilla. You need something extra to make it crazy and wild."

"Oh yeah? Like what? *You?*"

He raises his brow. "If that's what you think you need."

His smoldering eyes are watching me and I can tell they're thinking of doing naughty things. His charisma is absolutely magnetic.

Is my heartbeat racing? Because I feel hot all of a sudden. There's nothing I'd like to do more than jump Logan Drake's bones—to touch that body of his, to see if we have that sexual chemistry he's talking about, even though I know it's completely inappropriate.

"Absolutely not," I say. "We have a professional working relationship."

"You're right. We're professionals." He smirks as he takes a sip of beer.

I swallow. Just imagining him—naked—doing these things is insanely distracting.

"How many partners have you had?" He asks.

"Well." I clear my throat. "Keith is the only person I've ever slept with and we only did it once."

"No wonder you think sex is overrated. You did it with a guy who doesn't look like he knows what a shower is."

I laugh.

"Seriously though, why him? You guys don't seem like a match."

"I knew school would take up all my time, so I told myself not to date anyone."

"Why not?"

"It's too distracting. Relationships are a lot of work. Look at us." I lean in and lower my voice. "We're in a fake one and it's still a lot of work."

"Is this work?"

"You know what I mean." I sigh. "Anyway, I didn't date all through high school."

"What changed?"

"I turned twenty-one and I realized that if I don't date—or even lose my virginity—until the end of university, then I'd be in my late twenties! And isn't university all about gaining experience?"

"So you found the sleaziest guy you could?"

"No," I say defensively. "I was afraid to lose my virginity to the guy I actually liked—you know, in case I embarrassed myself. I didn't find the sleaziest guy, I found the easiest guy."

He bursts out laughing. "Okay, now it all makes sense."

I knit my eyebrows together. "It's not funny! I just wanted to get it over with and get all my nerves out of the way so that when I finally do it with someone I like, it will be good and amazing."

"How do you know it'll be good and amazing?"

"Because…you're going to find this silly." I look up at him.

"I won't, I promise."

"Because the next person I have sex with will be someone I'm in love with."

"And that'll make it better?"

"Of course!" I'm almost offended that he even has to ask. "I want more than just something physical…I want passion, intimacy, friendship, romance."

"Be prepared to be disappointed again." He drinks his beer.

"Have you ever had something like that?"

"Not really."

"And you don't think you ever will?"

He pauses. "I don't know."

"Well one day you might experience it and you'll think about me."

He laughs. "You want me to think of you when I'm having sex?"

"No!"

"Sorry—I meant *making love*."

"That's not what I mean."

He laughs again. "I know, I know. I'm just teasing you. You know, you're really cute when you're all romantic like this."

I sit up in my seat. "You don't believe in love?"

He leans in. "Now we're getting to the serious questions."

"You're deflecting."

"Have you ever been in love?"

In an effort to end this conversation, I look around the bar at all the students who are drinking and talking. Some are dancing on the makeshift dancefloor in front of the bar. When I look back at Logan, I'm struck by his dark eyes.

"You're staring at me again," I say.

"Your eyes. They remind me of the beach."

"The beach?"

"They're the color of sea glass. I used to go to the beach with my mom and brothers on holidays and we'd look for sea glass in the sand. The grayish-green of your eyes reminds me of that."

I smile.

"What?" He asks.

"The thought of you looking for sea glass on the beach with your mom and brothers is so wholesome. It's so different from what I envisioned you were like as a kid."

"And what do you think I was like?"

"A trouble-maker. You know, causing mischief everywhere you go. Cutting class. Breaking hearts."

He shrugs as he leans back. "I was a bit of both."

"No surprise there."

We both laugh.

My glasses slip down my nose. I push them back up.

"It's cute when you do that," he says.

Speechless, I ignore his compliment.

After all that beer and all that talk about sex, my body is singing.

No falling for him, I remind myself.

But things get more complicated when an Ed Sheeran song comes on and he asks me to dance.

"I don't think that's a good idea," I say.

"You're a good dancer. Come on."

He's impossible to resist. He takes my hand and I follow him onto the dance floor.

Pressing against his hard body, I wrap my arms around his neck. As I look up at him, I inhale his powerful masculine scent which makes me want to bury my face in his chest.

"Are you okay?" He asks.

No, I'm only a bit lightheaded and completely starstruck by you.

I nod. "I'm perfectly fine."

I'm in trouble.

12

LOGAN

Riley moves her body against mine and I can tell that she has good rhythm. My hands move over the curves of her waist as we dance. We're so close I can smell the cinnamon and beer on her breath. Her eyes look straight into mine.

Something about her lights a fire inside me. I don't know what it is. Maybe it's her no-nonsense attitude or her sharp wit. Or that everything has to be efficient with her, even her sex life. She's definitely the blue to my red.

Looking into those gray sea glass eyes, I know what I want to do.

But I can't. She's said so many times. Even though her hazy, seductive eyes seem to be telling me a different truth.

Her lips part.

"I think we should kiss," she whispers into my ear. Her arms are wrapped around me and she's so close, it feels like we're in our own little world. The rest of the people in the bar are a million miles away.

"You do?" My heart thumps hard against my chest.

"Yes," she breathes. "You know, for appearances."

"Oh."

"It'd be weird if we were on a date and we *didn't* kiss, right?"

I nod. "Right. Okay."

She hesitates for half a second before leaning in, connecting her soft velvet lips against mine. I taste the apple cinnamon on her lips. Pressing into her, I kiss her back. Her hand finds its way into my hair as she gets lost in the kiss. And, truthfully, so do I.

I let out an involuntary moan which causes her to pull back.

She clears her throat. "Well, now that that's out of the way…" She looks everywhere but at me. I watch her with intense curiosity, causing her eyes to lock with mine again. The chemistry between us lingers in the air.

"You're a really good kisser," I say. And I mean it.

She smiles. Time slows down as she leans in and presses her lips against mine again. This time I take my time kissing her. Her hands roam through my hair as she pulls me tighter against her. Her lips are soft and inviting, and her tongue teases mine. I start to forget that this is all for show.

"LAST CALL!"

Riley pulls away from me. "Oh crap. It's late. I have class in the morning."

"Let me walk you back to your building."

"Are you sure?" Every time we make eye contact, she pulls her gaze away.

My stomach sinks. Maybe that kiss wasn't real. What else would I expect from someone who's all about efficiency? Of *course* the kiss was fake.

"Of course," I say.

When we step outside, we discover it's pouring rain.

"Damn!"

"It doesn't look like it's letting up," I say.

"Let's just make a run for it."

"Really? Ms. Granola Bar wants to run through the rain?"

She gives me a sideways glance. "You got any better ideas?"

I shake my head. "Let's go, then."

We start running and we instantly get soaked. I try to shield her from the rain but it's coming down too hard and she's running too fast. When we reach her building, we're both drenched.

"Over here!" She says as she takes my hand.

We're both laughing as she pulls me into the elevator. Two other girls in the elevator are staring at us.

Riley's blouse is clinging to her body and I can tell she's cold. I hold her tight against me to warm her up. The other girls giggle and whisper to each other. I ignore them and look back down at Riley. She's smiling and, even though she's dripping wet, she looks beautiful.

We get off on her floor and I walk her to her door.

"Well, Mr. Drake," she says as she turns around, leaning back against her door. "Thank you for a fun evening."

"Same to you." I hover over her for a few seconds, waiting to see if she'll make a move for another kiss.

"Remember our rules," she whispers. "Displays of affection are only allowed if they're public."

There's that crushing disappointment again.

"I didn't realize you were such an exhibitionist," I say in a joking tone.

She chuckles. "I'm into a lot of things but that's not one of them."

I raise my eyebrows. "You're into a lot of things? As my fake girlfriend, do you care to share?

"Sorry, Mr. Drake. I only talk about my S&M preferences on the third fake date."

I laugh. "You're full of surprises."

"More than you know."

"I guess we have no choice but to go on that next date to find out."

She smiles as she turns the doorknob. "Good night, Logan Drake."

"Good night, Riley Jamieson." I take her hand and kiss it, looking up into her electric eyes. She smiles shyly as she pulls away, closing the door.

As I catch a ride home, I think about the evening. I've never had a date not end in sex. But I've also never had a date that left me with this much excitement stirring in my chest.

Either there's something between us, or she's a really good actress. No matter what the answer is, I know one thing for sure: I had a really good night.

13

RILEY

The next morning I'm in bed staring at the ceiling. I'm in a hazy cloud of being hungover and feeling high from the kiss.

I can't believe I did that.

What's wrong with me? I'm the one who was trying to keep things PG and yet I'm the one who kissed him.

But it felt so good.

I blame the sexually charged conversation and the beer.

Getting to know each other, my ass.

"Hey you." Jane is standing at her full-length mirror as she brushes her long dark hair. She's in a beautiful pink blouse and jeans. She looks way too good for going to an early morning class. I suddenly feel frumpy sitting in bed in my sweat pants and worn-out Beyonce t-shirt. "Why are you smiling?"

"I'm thinking about Logan."

I can see her wicked smile through the mirror's reflection. "You're in *loooove*."

"Oh, Jane, this is so messy."

"Messy in a good way?" She's pinning up her hair.

I shake my head. "I kissed him."

"Yum!"

"No, not yum. I didn't mean to."

She narrows her eyes. "You're dating him but you don't want to kiss him? Unless you're extremely religious or in a fake relationship with him, I don't—" Her eyes grow wide. "Oh my *god*."

"Jane, no—" I get out of bed and put my hands up, trying to coax the thought out of her. "What I mean is—"

"You…you used the app!"

"No, I didn't!" It's a lie and we both know it.

"This relationship is *fake*."

The word feels like a stab to my heart.

"Don't lie to me, Riley. I can see it in your eyes." She has a triumphant smile on her face.

"Fine, yes. It's fake."

Jane brings her hands to her mouth. "This is amazing!"

"No, it's embarrassing." I fall back into bed and cover my eyes in shame.

"No, no it's not. This is great! We're in this together now." Jane sits on the edge of my bed. "So, you kissed him? I haven't even kissed Rupert."

I nod. "Is that bad?"

She shrugs. "I don't know. Do you think it's bad? Did he kiss you back?"

"Oh yeah, he *definitely* kissed me back. And it's really bad because it's *so* good."

"Wow. You really like him. Like, *like* like."

I furrow my brow. "I'm annoyed that I understood that."

"Do you think he likes you?" She's staring at me with her big blue eyes.

"I don't know." I sigh. "The chemistry, the kiss. It all just seems so real."

"Do you think you can cancel the contract?"

"Cancel the—" I sit up and look at her. "I can't do that! I actually do need the money. And he's already given me most of it. What am I supposed to do? Give it back?"

She purses her lips. "Well, maybe he'll let you keep it?"

"Ugh." I rub my face. "Oh, Jane, I'm supposed to be focusing on school, not Logan Drake. I have so many projects coming up and I need to get really good grades if I want any of those job positions."

"Girl, you're in trouble."

"I know." I shake my head. "I can't believe I did that."

"I can. The man is *fine*."

"Oh my god, you have no idea. He's attractive, charming, and funny. He's a great dancer. *And* a great kisser. We just click together. It doesn't make any sense."

"You've got it bad, girl." Jane smirks as she braids her dark hair.

"Things are going to be so awkward between us."

"No, no, no. It doesn't have to be. When's the next time you see him?"

I think for a moment as I try to remember what day it is. Have I really been that thrown off my schedule?

"Tomorrow," I say finally. "We're going to a family skate function for the Blades."

"Pretend it never happened. Just act like it was part of the job."

I nod. "Yeah. PDA *is* part of our contract. Even though it felt so real."

Jane watches me wistfully. "I'm so jealous. All Rupert's ever done is kiss me on the cheek."

"Don't be jealous. This is more confusing than anything I've learned in school so far."

She sighs as she gets up and gathers her books. "Well, enjoy it while it lasts. Meanwhile, I've got to get to class. Talk to you later?"

"Yeah, later."

During my long day of classes, I think about Logan non-stop throughout the day.

The waitress from last night is sitting in the row in front of me during my last class. She gives me a bored look before talking loudly to her friend.

"You know who I served last night? Logan Drake."

"What?" Her friend asks. "Oh my god. *The* Logan Drake? He's *so* hot."

"I was disappointed," the waitress says. "He's not as flirty as the rumors say he is."

I can't help but smile as I flip open my notes.

Oh yes he is, I think to myself. *Yes, he is.*

***

The next day I meet Logan at the Blades arena for the family event. He's waiting at the entrance for me wearing casual jeans and a comfy blue sweater. His dark hair is casually pushed back. He's even more handsome than I remember. When he sees me, he smiles and butterflies dance in my belly.

"Hey," I say awkwardly.

"Hey," he says and, to my surprise, he leans in and kisses me on the cheek.

I awkwardly try to kiss him back. Fuck.

He takes my hand. "I hope you're ready to skate."

"As long as we don't drink any beer, I'll be fine."

He chuckles. "I hope our night of debauchery didn't affect your day yesterday."

"Nope, not at all," I lie. "So where do we lace up?" I gloss over the night completely.

Logan watches me with knowing eyes and a smirk.

"This way." He leads me into the arena where I see the rest of the team skating on the ice with their partners and kids. Music is playing and it feels like a real party. There's a large banner over the ice welcoming the friends and families of the Blades institution.

That familiar cold feeling washes through me as I look at all the people I have to lie to.

"I'm not sure I can do this," I say as I pull on Logan's hand. "What if we mess up?"

"Impossible."

"How can you be so confident?"

"Because we already have a pretty good relationship." He pushes a strand of hair behind my ear.

I lower my voice. "You're paying me."

"Yeah, but we have chemistry. That's why this is going to work so well." He smiles again.

Good lord, I really want to kiss him.

We strap our skates on and step onto the ice.

"Let's see what you've got, Jamieson." He takes my hands as if I'm a toddler learning to walk. But as soon as I step onto the ice, I glide effortlessly. He lets go of my hand as I do a triple turn. When I face him again his mouth is hanging open.

"I didn't know you knew how to skate," he says, dumbfounded.

"There's a lot of things you don't know about me, Mr. Drake." I wink.

He grabs my hand and pulls me around the rink for a few laps. Every once in a while, he puts his arm around my waist and spins me around. He tries to do something fancy and instead we both fail spectacularly. He falls back, pulling me down with him. Luckily, he cushions my fall.

"My bad," he says. We both laugh. His arms are around me, keeping me warm against him. I look into his eyes.

This would be a perfect time to kiss him, I think to myself.

And why not? We're in public and that's part of the contract.

Before I have a chance to kiss him, he takes the initiative and does it first. His soft, velvety lips press against mine. Before I even have a chance to appreciate how warm, how inviting his lips are, the kiss is over and I'm blinking absently at him.

Damn. We really do have chemistry.

Still processing what just happened, I get back onto my feet, pulling Logan up with me.

"Come on," he says. "Let me introduce you to some of my friends." He pulls me across the ice where we meet several members of the team. I pretend I've never heard of them as I shake their hands and feign learning their names. I'm also introduced to several of the girlfriends.

A bubbly blond named Marsha grabs my arm. "It's so nice to meet you! Come! Meet the rest of the girls."

She pulls me away as I make eye contact with Logan. He smiles as Marsha drags me toward the end of the rink with the other girls and introduces me to everyone.

"I'm Skip's girlfriend," Marsha says. Skip McGovern is the goalie for the Blades.

"I can't believe Logan has a girlfriend!" A woman with dark, frizzy hair says. Her name is Charlotte. "Tell me all about how you met."

I go over the story with them.

"That is *fantastic,*" Marsha says. "You're going to fit right in here."

"It's crazy," Charlotte says. "We never thought Drake would date anyone."

"He never dates *anyone,*" Marsha echoes.

"I heard he doesn't even let women sleep in his own bed," another one says.

"If he's bringing you to events like this it means he really likes you. Tell us, was it love at first sight?"

I bite my lip. Looking around at the anxious faces waiting for my answer, I nod. "Of course."

Was it?

The women squeal. "I knew it! You guys are *perfect* for each other. The way he looks at you—you can't fake that."

I smile absently as I stare at Logan who is skating around the rink with some kids. He looks up at me, giving me that attractive smile that makes me melt every time. "Right," I say. "You can't fake that."

"You're so great, Riley." Marsha squeezes my arm again. "We're so glad you're a part of our team!"

"Me too." My eyes are on Logan. "Me too."

14

LOGAN

"The sharks are circling," Marcus says.

We're hanging out by the boards near the table of coffee and bagels. We're both watching as five women are grilling Riley.

"Hey, are you alright?" Marcus waves his hand in my face. "You're very preoccupied right now."

"It's nothing."

But it's not nothing. It's something. All I can think about is that kiss. It was so instinctual, so automatic. I looked into her eyes and I felt like she was inviting me to do it. It all happened so fast. *And I want to do it more.*

"I saw that kiss," Marcus says. "You must really like her, huh? First the gallery, now this." Marcus dips a piece of sesame bagel into his coffee.

"We're getting along pretty well." I look back at Riley. She's skating in circles. "She's funny, smart, sweet. She's different."

How could I *not* kiss her when she's looking so cute in those jeans and those white skates?

Marcus laughs. "I can't believe this! Logan Drake—the eternal bachelor. The guy who used to have a drunken, naked photo in the tabloids every other week." He takes a big bite of his coffee-soaked bagel.

"Oh, come on. It wasn't *that* often. And besides, I don't think Riley would ever do that to me."

Marcus looks around and leans in. "Listen, don't get your heartbroken."

I wrinkle my brow. "What do you mean?"

"She's from an app, right?"

My heart squeezes in my chest. "Err—what are you talking about?"

"Spinner suggested it for me a few months ago. He suggested it for you too, didn't he? Hiring a fake girlfriend? It's kind of his go-to move for issues like this."

I don't say anything. Instead, I simply look into Marcus' eyes, trying to figure out if he's about to use that information against me, but all I see is kindness and a tinge of worry.

"Don't fall in love," he says. "She's only with you for the paycheck. Don't forget that."

"I—" I'm about to argue with him when I realize he's right. I'm hiring Riley. I paid off her tuition. *Obviously* that's why she's being so flirty with me in public. That's why she kissed me back. My stomach sinks. Even though my attraction for Riley seems to be growing with every passing minute, I can't risk blurring the lines between fantasy and reality because once they're blurred, they risk disappearing completely.

I sigh internally. Why did I put myself in this situation? Am I really this self-sabotaging?

"And don't let anyone find out," Marcus continues. "Journalists do *not* like being duped. They will drag you in all their papers."

"Nothing I haven't dealt with before."

"And they'll never vote for you for any award again."

I sigh. "Right."

"You *need* to keep this under wraps."

"I will. And you won't tell anyone, right?"

"Of course not." Marcus grabs another bagel and takes a bite causing a cascade of poppy seeds to tumble down the front of his shirt. "Trust me, don't mess this up."

"Hey." I furrow my brow. "When's the last time I messed something up?"

Marcus slaps me on the back. "Good joke, buddy."

"Seriously though," I answer back. "Have you seen our stats lately? *I'm* not the one messing up."

"Those are fighting words." Marcus pushes me strong enough to send me down the ice. "Bet you can't get two points next game."

I skate back towards him. "You're on."

Someone calls out for Marcus and he skates away. I stare across the ice at Riley again. She's showing one of the kids how to do a spin.

She wouldn't hurt me like some of the other women I've dated. She wouldn't take photos of me naked to humiliate me in exchange for money. She wouldn't sabotage me for her own gain. Deep down, she respects me. She may even like me.

I catch her eye and she smiles before skating over to me.

"How am I doing?" She asks as she stops in front of me.

"I knew you'd get along great with everyone."

She puts her arm around my waist. The intoxicating smell of her apple shampoo surrounds me.

"Race you around the rink?" She asks.

"You think you can out-skate me?"

"Duh." She pushes off the ice and begins skating without any kind of warning. I smile to myself as I chase after her.

I'm not gonna mess this up.

15

RILEY

Over the next week, I get a break from girlfriend duty as Logan travels out of town for a few games. It's a welcome break as I get to forget about my crush on Logan and those two kisses we shared — one at the bar and one at the ice rink. I know that if I had to be around him any longer, I wouldn't be able to hide my attraction to him. Or what I think is my attraction to him.

Things are getting so complicated that I don't even know where our fake relationship ends and reality begins. That's why Logan being out of town is such a relief. Being able to forget about all that and focus on school work is a *very* welcome distraction.

The semester is winding down and the work is piling up, forcing me to spend all my free time in the library working. The rain has been coming down hard outside all week, making a great soundtrack for studying. I'm grateful for the hiatus but I still can't help myself from noticing that he should be back either today or tomorrow. I keep pausing between study breaks to see if he's messaged me.

Gosh, I'm pathetic.

I can't even go out on several fake dates without turning to goo. I console myself with the fact that this isn't just any man. It's Logan Drake. I've replayed the past few weeks over and over in my head, fantasizing about all the things we would have done together if these were real dates.

Am I crazy?

Yes. Absolutely. And I only get crazier as the day when Logan returns draws near. I keep expecting him to message me, to tell me he needs me to go to another event with him, but nothing comes.

Distracted from school work, I dig into my wallet looking for the contract. After checking the usual pocket I use, I'm perplexed to find it in the pocket where I keep my money. I must've put it in there without realizing back at the gala. It's just another sign that I'm completely distracted by Logan. Pulling the folded piece of paper out carefully so nobody in the library around me can read over my shoulder, I unfold it. The sight of Logan's signature grounds me in reality.

None of this is real, I remind myself. It's all fake. The PDA, the laughter on the ice rink, even the kisses. Everything is fake.

Swallowing past the lump in my throat, I put the contract away and chip away at my mountain of homework.

When the sky gets dark and the library is mostly empty, I put my books away, grab my umbrella, and make my way out into the pouring rain to navigate my way to the residence building. Terry, one of the floor managers, is in the lobby pinning bright pink flyers onto the cork-board.

"You're still here?" He asks.

"Yeah, why? What's up?" I look around at all the wet-floor signs everywhere.

"The rain has been flooding through the building since this morning," he says. "Only a few of the rooms are in the flood path but it could get worse. The whole building's being evacuated."

"Oh, damn!"

"That's right."

"So, what do they want us to do? Sleep in a hotel?" I shift the bag of books which are pulling on my shoulder. My socks are still wet from the rain.

"Most people have been relocated to the empty rooms in the residence building across campus, but I think all the rooms have been taken. You'll have to find your own place to stay."

"That's it? No compensation?"

He hands me one of his pink flyers. "You can call university admin on here but it might be a few days before they find a place for you."

"Ugh, that sucks."

He shrugs. "Student life, am I right? You've got an hour before the building is roped off completely."

He takes his flyers and sets off down the hallway.

Mumbling to myself, I take the stairs up to my room (which thankfully hasn't been affected by the flooding yet) and find my small suitcase. Jane is out of town visiting her parents, so I'm on my own. I look down at the pink flyer which is breaking apart in my wet hands.

"Shit."

What am I going to do?

I'm not broke anymore. I could stay at a hotel. Maybe somewhere with a good desk for studying. As I grab some clean clothes and notebooks, I see my Blades jersey. As I pick up my phone, another idea forms in the back of my mind. I know I shouldn't even be entertaining that idea, and it goes against every rule in our contract, but I can't help myself. Grabbing my phone, I text Logan.

***

With my small suitcase in hand, I make my way to Logan's place. His place is located up in the hills. I've heard that the condos up there are expensive but I'm absolutely floored when I see them in person.

The square condo sits on the hill overlooking a sea of city lights. The condo itself looks like a futuristic castle up on the hill. A beautiful garden surrounds it and I'm sure it's even more beautiful when it's not raining.

I make my way inside the lobby area which is decorated with art and beautiful plants. I look around. There are two doors—one for the lower-level apartment and one for the elevator. As I make my way toward the elevator, I hear an old voice.

"Are you a friend of Logan's?"

I turn to see a wrinkled lady who barely stands taller than five feet.

I nod. "Yes. I'm Riley."

"Oh, I've heard about you." She winks at me.

"You have?"

She must read the papers.

"Yes. Logan talks about you."

"He does?" I try not to sound so shocked, but I can't help myself.

He talks about me?

"Oh, yes. I'm Madeline, by the way. Logan's neighbor."

"Nice to meet you, Madeline."

"You know, he's such a kind man. I'm glad he's finally dating someone. He's been so lonely since he moved here."

He hasn't had *any* women come by since he's moved here? *Interesting.*

"Here." Madeline shuffles toward the elevator. "Let me call the elevator for you."

"Thank you."

I make my way into the elevator and up to Logan's apartment. As the elevator lurches up, I think about how surreal it is that I'm about to step into Logan Drake's apartment. The doors open and I step inside.

The place is just as impressive as I was expecting it to be. The open concept kitchen and living room area is sleek and modern, straight out of a magazine. On the opposite wall is a large window looking out over the city. The view of the twinkling lights is absolutely breathtaking.

Unable to help myself, I peek around. Although I've been on three fake dates with Logan, this is the most intimate view of him that I've seen so far. I get to see the silver, black, and blue accents of his furniture and décor—Seattle Blades colors through and through. I'm surprised by his chic and modern style. Everything is much nicer and tidier than I expected.

To my right, I see the bedroom door open. I step inside and look at the king-sized bed, which looks insanely comfortable. Walking around his room, I see the large walk-in closet. I step inside. There's a long rack where all his suits and old jerseys are hanging. I brush my hand over them, feeling the material of each one. His intoxicating masculine scent lingers throughout the closet.

Without caring to hold myself back, I lean into one of his suit jackets, bury my nose in the material, and inhale. It smells overwhelmingly like Logan.

"God, I have no shame. And no self-control."

Leaving the closet before I do something dumb, I continue toward what has to be the master bathroom on the opposite side of the room. Curious to see what a millionaire's bathroom looks like, I get closer to investigate. The door is almost closed and as I pull the door open, I see light and movement. The water is running. I freeze.

He's already home.

Though I don't mean to, I catch a glimpse of him in the glass shower. Through the steam, I see the curved muscles of his backside.

Oh my god! I swing the door shut. Heart racing in my chest, I step back through the bedroom and make my way out into the living room.

With my cheeks feeling like they're on fire, I stifle my laughter.

Hoping that he didn't notice me, I feign interest in the shelves around the large flat screen TV. The shelves are filled with gold trophies of all sizes. It's no secret that Logan is amazing at hockey. Apparently, he needs constant reminding.

A framed photo is placed face down next to the television. I look around to make sure I'm alone before picking it up. It's a picture of Logan and Harrison Cooper playing ball hockey on the street. They both look young, about nine or ten years old, and full of joy. It's a rare glimpse into the history of two of hockey's greatest players.

After I place the frame back down where I found it, my eyes drift to a framed photo hanging on the wall. Logan is about fifteen in this photo. He's sitting on a couch with two guys and an older woman. They're all smiling and laughing. Both guys are about the same age as Logan, the same size and build too. The woman is older but full of life. They all have those familiar dark eyes.

"My mother," A deep voice says, causing me to jump.

I turn to face Logan. He's wearing low-waisted jeans and a form-fitting black t-shirt. His towel-dried hair is wavy and looks like he's run his hands through it a few times. I breathe in his clean masculine scent.

"She's beautiful," I say.

"She's a good mom."

"And those are your brothers?"

"Kevin and Mark. They're older than me. I've always been the baby of the family."

"You all look so similar."

"Trust me, I'm cuter."

"Are you sure?" I look back at the photo. "Because Mark is pretty cute."

He smirks. "You like giving me a hard time, don't you?"

I smile. "It makes life a bit more fun."

He watches me with a keen eye that almost draws me in.

Regaining my composure, I look at the picture again. "Where are your brothers now?"

"Kevin plays football in Florida. Mark is in law school in Chicago."

"Living with two older brothers must've been fun."

"We were pretty competitive. They have a few years on me, so I was always picked on."

"I'm sure your mom was thrilled to have three sons."

He laughs. "Thrilled isn't the word she'd use. But she loves us. My dad left when we were young, so she raised us on her own."

"Oh, I'm so sorry."

"It's fine. I never really knew him anyway." He catches my eye. "Don't look at me like that."

"Like what?"

"All sad and stuff. We're a happy family. They're my everything. Plus, my brothers and I are all doing pretty good for ourselves."

I smile and look back at the picture. "Your mom must be happy that all three of you are very successful."

"Well, we're not successful until we give her lots of grandbabies. That's what she wants."

"Is that what you want?" The question escapes my lips before I realize what I'm asking.

"Maybe one day. I wouldn't mind having a baby or two. We'd live in a big house. I could teach them how to skate, how to play hockey."

I'm momentarily thrown off by his use of 'we'.

"What about you?" He asks.

Although I never really thought about kids and spent most of my years thinking about my career, hearing Logan Drake talk about his dreams of having children makes me feel all warm and fuzzy inside.

"A few kids would be nice," I say. "You could teach them how to skate and I'll teach them how to study."

He smiles. "I meant, what's your family like?"

"Oh." My cheeks get hot quickly. "My family is—" I'm about to say 'boring' but I realize how insensitive that would sound. If interesting means having a rocky past like Logan's, then I'll take boring any day of the week. "My family is small. It used to feel bigger when Aunt Mary was still with us but now it's just me and my parents. They live in Portland."

Logan watches me with a lingering stare. "They must be very proud of you."

I smile. "They are."

His gaze lingers and I feel the tension tightening between us. His brown eyes pull me in.

I clear my throat in an attempt to diffuse the mounting tension.

"What's this?" I grab the frame that I know has the picture of him and Cooper in it. I pretend that I'm seeing it for the first time by pointing out how adorably cute he is and poking fun at his neon green knee-high socks.

"I meant to put that away" He grabs the frame out of my hands.

"Why? Don't you think you two will make up eventually?"

"I don't know." He stares at the picture. "I want to."

"Why don't you reach out to him? If you want to be friends again, why not speed up the process?"

"I don't know." He rubs the back of his neck, giving me a nice view of his toned arms. "I'm not that kind of guy, you know?"

"What kind of guy are you?"

He drops his arm, causing the masculine scent of his deodorant to push out into the air around us. He looks at his trophies on the shelf nearby. "I'm a competitor," he says.

"Competitors don't make the first move to make up with their friends? Why not be competitive with friendship?"

He laughs gently. "Well, we'll see. Do you always play therapist with your friends?"

I smirk. "So, we're officially friends. Am I going to get my picture up on the wall any time soon?"

He smiles. "We've been friends since the beginning."

"Maybe not *right* at the beginning. We had a pretty rocky start."

He laughs. "That's true. I think we're doing okay now."

"Enjoy it while it lasts. You'll be sick of me in a few days."

"Impossible. It'd take a lot for me to get sick of you." He smirks and it stirs something inside me.

His masculine scent suddenly feels overwhelming. I break the eye contact between us and look around the living room, pretending I don't notice that he's still staring at me. "So where can I sleep? Does the couch turn into a bed?"

He points to the bedroom. "You can put your stuff in there."

My heart squeezes. "You want me to stay in your bedroom?"

"Well, you can stay on thc couch but it's just a couch. I mean, it's a pretty damn comfortable couch, but the bed is more comfortable. I know you need a good rest when you're studying, so I figured you should take it."

"But you also need good rest when you're playing hockey."

"True. I mean, we can sleep together if you like. The bed's big enough for the two of us. It's bigger than a king. Custom made." He says this so nonchalantly that I accidently bite my tongue.

"Umm." God knows I want to, but it'd be completely inappropriate. Our relationship is professional no matter how friendly, or flirty, we are with each other behind closed doors. I realize that my very pregnant pause is about to give birth. I need to give him an answer. *Now.* "You just *have* to suggest something completely inappropriate that goes against all the contract's rules, didn't you?"

He smirks. "I'm the bad boy sex maniac of hockey, aren't I?"

I roll my eyes but I can't help but smile.

"I'm surprised, Mr. Drake. I expected you to make fun of me for bringing up the contract, but instead you went the self-deprecating route."

He shrugs. "What can I say? I'm full of surprises."

"You really are. Honestly, I didn't even expect your apartment to look this nice."

"What were you expecting? Lego pieces all over the floor?"

"More like posters of half-naked women and empty condom wrappers."

He grabs his chest as if his heart is breaking. "You've gotta give me more credit than that!"

"I mean, I do now," I say as I look around at the minimalist decor and immaculately clean kitchen. "But I at least expected an Xbox."

"Ask and you shall receive." He opens a cabinet under the television to reveal his gaming station. "Do you play?"

"They have one in the student lounge. I play sometimes. It depends on what games you've got."

"I'll show you my collection and maybe we can battle after dinner."

"Sure. But I warn you, I won't make it easy on you."

He laughs. "I didn't expect you to talk such a big game."

"I don't just talk it."

He raises his eyebrows. "Oh, okay. I see how it is. How about I start preparing dinner so that I can make you eat your words."

There's something sexy about a guy who isn't afraid to be competitive. My A-type personality is constantly looking for competition, but men often avoid me. Whether it's because they don't want to offend a woman, I don't know. But Logan's competitiveness is refreshing.

"Do you like lasagna? I know it's a bit crazy for someone who only eats granola bars."

I laugh. "You mean you're not serving me bland protein shakes the entire time I'm here?"

"I want to see if you can handle some spice." He gives me a devious glance.

"Oh, I can handle some spice."

"Good." He smirks. "Come join me in the kitchen. You can be my sous-chef."

"Okay, but only if I don't have to wear one of those weird chef hats."

"I make no promises." He gives me a handsome smile. He doesn't even have to put effort in. He just has to look at me and I melt.

"I'll put my stuff away and then I'll come join you." I grab my suitcase.

"Oh, by the way" he says, catching my attention. "Next time you catch me showering, just leave the door open a bit. I don't like it getting too steamy in there."

Oh god.

"Right. Sorry."

My skin instantly feels hot as I squeeze my eyes shut and turn away, rushing into Logan's room. As I close the door behind me, I collapse in embarrassment onto his bed.

16

LOGAN

"It's been great so far. She's usually at school, I'm at practice. But we had enough time to spend one night talking about *everything*. Get this, we both have the same dream to travel to the Grand Canyon."

Marcus and I are walking down the arena hallway to the locker room before that night's game.

"So?" Marcus asks. "What's the problem?"

"She's driving me crazy."

"If it's driving you crazy, ask her to leave."

"No," I say a little too forcefully. "I mean, she's driving me crazy in a good way. The way she laughs. And she smells *amazing*"

"Then tell her that."

"I can't."

"Why not?"

I pause. "What if she doesn't like me?"

"Dude, she wouldn't be staying with you if she didn't like you."

"I told you, her dorm building flooded."

Marcus watches me with raised eyebrows. "Seriously? You don't think she could afford the fancy hotel with all that contract money?"

"*Shh.*" I look around.

"Just tell her how you feel. It's a hell of a lot better than moping around like this."

I shake my head. "I can't do that."

"Well, get your damn head in order because we have an important game tonight. If we win, we could gain a four-point swing. Our chances of going to the playoffs will be a lot easier."

"I know." I shake my head, trying to shake the thoughts of Riley away.

Six guys from the Cleveland Crushers appear down the hallway.

"If we lose tonight, they qualify for the playoffs," I say.

From across the hall, I see a familiar face. Harrison Cooper is in his favorite blue suit as he walks with the rest of the team toward the visiting team's locker room.

"Hey, isn't this the first time you're playing against the Crushers since you got kicked off the team?" Marcus asks.

"Yeah," I mumble.

"Will you be okay?"

"Of course." I look at Marcus. "Why wouldn't I be?"

"You've got a bunch of relationship drama right now, dude."

I force out a laugh. "Let me fix some of it right now."

With Riley's words on my mind, I walk over to Coop.

"Hey," I say, grabbing his attention. Coop stares at me with a hardened face. His stern green eyes bring back memories of all the fights we had as teenagers, fights that were always solved with a cup of hot cocoa (a special Cooper family recipe). I stick out my hand, expecting a gentlemanly handshake. "I just want to say good luck tonight."

Coop looks down at my hand and pulls away. I stand in shock for a moment before turning back to Marcus.

"Still mad, I guess," he says.

"Yeah," I say absently as I watch Coop pull away with the rest of the team. This would need more than a cup of special hot cocoa.

"Don't feel too bad." Marcus pats me on the back and pulls me into our locker room. "Get back at him on the ice. No fighting though."

I smirk. "I can do that."

An hour later, we're standing at center ice facing Coop as we prepare to battle for the puck.

Coop and I facing off against each other has been huge news all week. The whole hockey world is watching this game tonight. I can practically hear everyone in the stadium holding their breath.

The referee drops the puck and without hesitation I snatch it away from Coop, passing it to Edgar on my right. We skate around the others and set up formation in the opposing end. Edgar passes it to me, I pass it back to him. The crowd gets loud. Edgar shoots! He misses. The goalie passes the puck to Coop who skates it up the ice, evading every player along the way. I push myself to keep up with him but he's always been the faster skater. He's in the zone. He winds up to take a shot. The puck is alone on the ice for a split second. Reaching my stick out, I pull it away from him.

Yes!

The crowd cheers louder.

Just as I'm about to skate to the other end, Coop steals the puck back from me and, in one sweeping motion, he scores. The other team is celebrating before I even get a chance to process what just happened.

"What the—"

Marcus pats me on the back. "Tough break, bud. He's just too fast."

"I guess so," I mumble to myself. Skating back to the bench, I sit on the end closest to the other team.

Coop fist-bumps everyone on his bench before hopping over the boards and sitting a few feet away from me.

"Hey," I shout over the boards, grabbing his attention.

He looks over at me.

"Good goal. You've still got those fast hands."

Hesitantly, he smiles. "Thanks."

I shift my attention back onto the ice. When the whistle blows to pause the play, I look up into the stands where the family and friends sit. I see Riley's blond head sitting on the end of the row. Even from the ice, I can tell she's touching her necklace, her good luck charm.

"Don't worry, buddy. We've got this," Marcus says. He squeezes my shoulder.

"I'm not worried," I say as I smile. My eyes are still on Riley. "I'm not worried at all."

17

RILEY

During the intermission, I'm standing near the concession stand getting a bag of popcorn with Shelly. A nearby horn signals that the game will be back on soon. As we make our way back to our seats, Shelly stops.

"Oh no," she says. "Look who it is."

A woman with jet black hair is sitting in the empty seat next to mine.

"Who is that?" I ask.

"That's Catherine," Shelly says.

The name stirs my heart as I recognize it immediately. Catherine is Harrison Cooper's girlfriend. She was the woman that came between him and Logan. She was the reason for their fight. *She was Logan's ex.*

Popcorn in hand, we squeeze into our row and find our seats which are being saved by our coats and bags.

As I sit down and slip my change into my bag, I sit back with my popcorn. Catherine clips me with her elbow as she leans on the armrest between us, making herself comfortable.

I try to ignore her and focus on the game which just started. I look for number thirteen.

"So." Catherine looks at me. She's close enough that I can feel her breath, which smells like lipstick. "You're Logan's friend?"

"We're dating," I say casually as I keep my eyes on the game.

She looks me up and down. "You?" She lets out a laugh. "No one dates Logan Drake. He's not a *dater*."

"What do you mean?" I finally pull my gaze to look into her green eyes which are made all the more vibrant by her dark raven hair. I wish I could say she was unattractive, but her beauty is striking.

Catherine shrugs dismissively. "He's just not a dater, that's all."

"Well, that's clearly not true because I'm dating him."

"Have you seen his place?" She asks as if she's a lawyer.

Is she on to me? Is she trying to trap me in a lie?

I sit up. "Not only have I seen his place, but I've also slept in his bed."

Her smile disappears. "No, you haven't. Logan Drake does *not* let women sleep in his bed. At least, he didn't let me..."

I smirk. "Where do you think I slept last night?"

She looks me up and down again while her nostrils flare. Leaning in, she asks, "How much are you making off of him?"

My blood freezes. *Does she know?* The last thing I need right now is for someone to spill the beans about us.

"One nude photo can make you a millionaire," she says under her breath.

Oh. So *that's* what she means. She wants me to blackmail him.

In the distance, a horn blares. The crowd erupts into cheers, but I'm locked in my seat staring at Catherine.

"How could you do this to someone?" I ask. "How can you live with yourself?"

She rolls her eyes. "These guys don't care about us. You're a fool to think they do."

"Logan and I are happy," I say. Deep down, I mean it.

She stares at me, seeming furious that Logan Drake could possibly have a relationship with me—the nerdy girl who lost her virginity to the campus clown.

She flips her hair. "Whatever. You don't get to judge me." She gets out of her seat and squeezes past everyone down the row until she disappears.

"What was her problem?" I ask.

"Ignore her," Shelly says. "She's a vulture."

I sit back in my seat and focus on the game, hoping to forget everything that just happened. But Catherine's words burrow deep. She's right. Logan is using me. But I'm not lying when I say I care about him.

I watch number thirteen as he speeds down the ice, putting the puck into the net. The crowd roars. Everyone is looking at him. Logan turns and looks up at me. He points in my direction as the arena rumbles around us.

***

The game ends with a come-from-behind win for the Cleveland Crushers. After a quick visit to the university to submit a project before the midnight deadline, I make my way back to Logan's place. As I make my way up to his apartment, I worry about how I'll find him. Will he be angry? Sulking? Depressed?

Whatever he's feeling, I can understand why. His former team, the Cleveland Crushers, made it into the playoffs. And his best friend Coop is still dating the woman who used blackmail to completely disrupt his career.

I prepare to comfort him, to be understanding and give him space if he needs it. But when I enter his apartment, I'm surprised to find him happily chopping tomatoes at the kitchen counter.

"Hey, pretty lady." He looks up at me and smiles. "You hungry?"

A delicious aroma is drifting out of the kitchen.

"There's a casserole in the oven and the timer is set to go off in fifteen minutes."

"Midnight casserole?"

"What can I say? I'm famished."

"You're in a good mood."

"I can't let that game get to me." He scrapes the chopped tomatoes into a bowl and starts cutting a red pepper. "We can still get enough points to qualify in the upcoming games. Which, by the way, I'm leaving tonight after dinner. Coach wants us there early so we can practice tomorrow morning.'

"But the Crushers," I say. "Your old team advanced to the playoffs."

"You know, it's weird," he says. "I thought this would be a bit more soul-crushing. But the truth is, I'm happy for Coop."

"You are?"

"Yeah. He played a good game. It was a good competition. And that's all we ever really wanted from each other."

"Oh, well color me impressed, Mr. Drake."

He smiles. "Besides…you gave me good advice about being the first one to reach out."

"You reached out to him?"

He puts the paring knife down and leans on the counter.

"I tried to. He's still mad but I felt good doing it. At least I tried, you know? So, thanks for that."

I smile. "You're welcome."

He keeps his gaze on me.

"What?"

"You were touching your necklace today."

My hand shoots up to my Aunt Mary's rose pendant. "I wanted you guys to have good luck."

He grins. "You *do* care about me."

"Of course, I do." I look into those dark eyes of his.

I could kiss him right now.

"You know…" His gaze lingers on me. "It's been really nice having you here."

"I've enjoyed being here…and it's too bad that I'll be leaving tomorrow."

"You are?" He furrows his brow.

"Yeah, well…the res building was cleared today so they're letting people back in tomorrow." I internally chastise myself for sharing all this information. I could have milked this scenario for a little bit longer.

"Oh. Okay." He looks back down at his cooking.

"You look sad," I say.

He smirks. "Not sad. I'm just wondering who I'm going to play Xbox with."

I smile. "You really want to get your ass kicked again?"

"Well, I'm getting better!"

I chuckle as I lean on the counter, unintentionally getting closer to him.

"I'm going to miss staying here. It was fun hanging out with you."

As he looks up at me with that seductive gaze, his dark hair falls into his eyes. "I'm going to miss you too."

Oh boy.

He's so close that I can smell his spicy, earthy scent. I inhale so deeply that I make myself a bit dizzy.

An overwhelming feeling comes over me. Throwing caution to the wind, I lean in and press my lips against his.

My body tenses for a moment but when I feel him kiss me back, I allow myself to relax and melt into him.

He runs his hand through my hair as he deepens the kiss. His lips are even plumper, more delicious than I remember. And, even though we've done this before, this feels different. This feels natural, organic. This feels like something more.

My hands move up his chest as he presses his body against mine. His hands slither around my waist. My knees threaten to buckle beneath me but I manage to remain stable.

I move my hands over his shoulders, his neck, up into his hair. I touch him the way I've wanted to touch him this whole time.

The world seems to disappear and time slows down completely as we lose ourselves in each other, releasing several weeks of tension like a dam releasing a river. Kissing him with intention, I respond to his pace.

I let out an involuntary moan as I come up for air.

Logan kisses my cheek, my neck. In an effort to breathe in his addictive aroma, I inhale… but I smell something burning instead.

"It's hot," I manage to say.

"Yes," he breathes.

"No, I mean. It's burning. The food is burning!" As much as I don't want this make-out session to end, I pull away from Logan and grab the oven mitts.

The alarm goes off.

BEEP! BEEP! BEEP!

"Oh shit!" Logan grabs a pan and starts fanning the alarm.

BEEP! BEEP! BEEP!

I pull the oven door open, allowing a dark plume of smoke to billow out.

BEEP! BEEP! BEEP!

I pull the crisp casserole out of the oven as Logan opens the windows.

"That's what I get for trying to make a nice meal!" Logan rushes over to survey the damage.

"Only part of it is burned. We can eat the rest!"

He laughs. "If you want to. I'll have the frozen pizza that's in the freezer."

"I think we'll be okay." I look up at him. His piercing dark eyes don't waver.

We stare at each other in silence.

"We kissed," I say, finally.

"Yes, we did," he says confidently.

My body feels like it's buzzing from head to toe. I barely have a chance to process what this all means when Logan leans in to kiss me again. His hands find their place on my waist. My body is pulsing with excitement. I've never felt this wild before.

A kiss. A kiss with no ulterior motives.

It almost feels unreal.

Just as we're about to get back into the rhythm of things, the doorbell rings.

Logan exhales heavily.

"That's my ride to the airport."

"You have to leave already?"

"Coach's orders." He sighs and leans his forehead against mine. "I just want to stay here and keep kissing you." He holds me tight against him.

"Me too. Or maybe I can crawl into your suitcase."

He laughs. "Coach wouldn't like that so much."

"That's too bad."

The doorbell rings again, and now Logan's phone is buzzing.

He smiles and nods over at the counter. "Enjoy that for me."

I look at the half-burnt casserole. "Maybe I'll have the pizza."

He kisses me again. "I'll talk to you later, Riley."

"Yeah," I say, still in a trance. "Later."

He grabs his jacket and the hockey bag next to the door. Giving me one last look, he smiles and leaves.

I look back at the food but all I can taste is Logan. He tastes like the best and worst decision of my life.

18

RILEY

"You're sleeping in his bed? You *kissed* him?" Jane and I are seated in the off-campus coffee shop. Our laptops and books are spread out all over the table. It's a nice break from the library since we can actually chat out loud. Since it's raining, the place is fairly empty. The only other person around is a hooded student quietly working on the other side of the room.

"I couldn't help myself. I can't resist him! He's literally irresistible." I take a sip of Brazilian dark roast. The mug is so big I need both hands.

"How did this happen?"

"Well, where do I start?" I put my mug down. "He's fun to be around. He's got deep feelings and a good heart. He's just…wonderful."

"And sexy."

"That too."

"And have you guys, you know…?" Jane smiles devilishly. Her curious eyes watch me carefully as if any subtle expression will give her the answer she's looking for.

My heart flutters at the thought of it. "No."

"But you want to." She grabs her glass of iced coffee and sips from a metal straw.

"Well, yeah. Who wouldn't?"

"Obviously everybody who has eyes and a libido. But this is different."

"How?"

She looks into my eyes. "You're sleeping in his bed. You *kissed* him. This means you like him. You *love* him."

"I—" I'm about to deny it but she's right.

"What do you think will happen between you two?"

"I don't know. We haven't spoken about it. He's been gone since it happened and it's not really something I want to talk about over text."

"Well, you guys ended the contract, right?"

The contract. Right. *Fuck.*

I bite my lip and give her an innocent shrug.

"Riley!" She puts her drink down and grabs my arm with her ice-cold hand. "You didn't end the contract?"

"Shh." I look around, making sure the hooded guy at the next table isn't listening. "What do I do?"

"Talk to him about it!"

"What if he doesn't like me that way?"

"He kissed you, didn't he?"

"Yeah, but that doesn't mean I can upgrade to his...*real girlfriend,*" I whisper those last words.

"What's the alternative? Not talk about it until the contract's up? That's just confusing and messy."

"I know." I rub my face. This was *not* the dilemma I needed on a day planned out for studying.

I look at my notes which are all color-coded and divided into sections based on half-hour work sessions. According to the schedule I pre-planned for myself, I'm already two sessions behind.

Damn you, Logan Drake. Quit distracting me from my schoolwork!

"Are we ready for another study session?" I ask.

"You're not really changing the subject that fast, are you?"

"This may come as a shock for you, but I actually do need to study during my study sessions."

Jane sighs. "Fine. But you can't just drop a bomb like that and expect me not to talk about it! This discussion isn't over."

I smirk.

Jane gets up. "Do you want more coffee before we start our session?"

"Yes, please." I hand over my massive mug.

Jane makes her way up to the counter, giving me a brief moment of privacy. Discretely grabbing my phone from my backpack, I check it under the table. I have a text from Logan. Just seeing his name makes my belly flip.

> LOGAN: I'm back in town at the end of the week. Come watch me play?

My eyes drift up to my color-coded study schedule. I'm already way too behind. I type back.

RILEY: I've got a ton of work to do.

LOGAN: The game's not until the end of the week. You've got plenty of time. Besides, the game won't be the same without my lady luck.

I smile. There's something extremely sexy about being his lady luck. There's something extremely sexy about being his *anything*.

Jane is walking back over with our drinks. I type quickly.

RILEY: Well, in that case, I'll try to get it all done in time.

Shoving my phone back into my pocket, I put it out of sight. I don't need any more distractions from Logan and I definitely don't need any prying from Jane.

"Here we are." Jane places the drinks on the table. "One iced coffee and a latte."

"Thank you, my hero."

"And before our session begins, I need to use the ladies room." Jane saunters away.

I look back at my notes. I manage to read two paragraphs before my mind drifts to Logan. I think about his lips, his hands around my waist, and the look in his eyes after we kissed. That wild, seductive stare that looked like he was ready to devour me right then and there.

My phone buzzes, vibrating against my thigh. I bite back a smile because I know it's him. I fish the phone out of my pocket.

God, I have zero self-control.

I look at the message. It's from Logan, as I expected. He sent me a happy face. I smile as I tuck my phone into my purse. Maybe I'll be less distracted if I keep it there instead. As I place the phone somewhere safe, my hand brushes against my wallet and I feel the sharp edges of the contract poking out. My fingers settle on the edges of the paper for a moment before I look back at my notes.

Two days until I see him. Two days until I ask him about it.

As I exhale, I pull my fingers from the contract, push Logan out of my mind, and direct my focus back on my work.

19

LOGAN

"Last game of the regular season," Marcus says. We're in the locker room getting ready for the game. "We win this and we get to the playoffs. It doesn't get crazier than this."

"Right," I say absently as I dig through my bag, looking for my phone.

Marcus looks at me as he wraps his stick with tape. "Are you even paying attention? Where's your head been?"

"It's here," I mumble. But it's not. I'm thinking about Riley. I've been away all week and I haven't seen her since we had that kiss the night I left. I'm finally back in Seattle and I can't stop thinking about all the things I want to do to her when I see her again.

As I fish out my phone, I notice there are no messages from Riley. It's not a surprise. She's been quiet all week, ever since we kissed. I still don't even know if she's out in the crowd watching the game tonight. Either way, being back in Seattle and so close to her is driving me crazy. I know I should be focused on the game tonight, but I can't help being more excited to see Riley. I need her like I need my next breath.

I'm about to put my phone away when I notice a notification from my hockey app.

"Crap."

"What is it?" Marcus looks up.

"Cooper scored three goals in today's game. He's leading me by a single point!"

Marcus pats me on the shoulder. "You know what to do."

The team cheers as we walk out onto the ice for our warmup. As I skate around, I casually look up at the family and friends area. There she is. Even in the giant arena, I feel Riley's presence like a glowing orange light. Just knowing she's there empowers me. As I skate, I feel like I'm gliding on air.

The game starts and it's an even match. We have trouble getting around their defense while they have trouble getting the puck to the net. This goes on for all three periods until all the guys are tired and frustrated and we're forced into overtime.

Coach pulls out a small whiteboard and pulls everyone in for a huddle. Sweating like crazy, I lean in. Only five minutes left to make it into the playoffs. Only five minutes and the game will be over, and I can be with Riley again. We can finish what we started. My eyes drift up to the crowd. I can see her blond head in the distance.

"Can you do that, boys?" Coach asks.

"Yeah!"

"Logan?"

I look up at him, realizing that I'm part of his overtime plan. "Yeah."

"Come on, let's do it!"

I hop over the boards and join Edgar and Marcus on the ice. As I skate around the rink, I look up at Riley again. Her hand is on her necklace.

Positioning myself at center ice, I ready my stick for the play. This is it. I need one more point to be on the same level as Cooper. I need one more point to help the Blades make it to the playoffs.

The referee drops the puck, which I immediately take control of and pass to Edgar. The two of us skate around the opposing players with ease.

Edgar passes it back to me as I enter their zone. An opposing player reaches around my legs for the puck but I hop over his stick and pass the puck up to Marcus, who passes it to Edgar, who passes it back to me with lightning speed.

In that same instant, I look up and see an empty space between the goalie's legs. The goalie is still looking at Edgar.

Without hesitation, I push the puck through the open slot, burying it in the back of the net. The goal light goes off and the arena erupts into cheers. Throwing my stick and gloves onto the ice, I throw my hands up and jump into Marcus' arms.

"We did it! We did it!"

"Playoffs here we come!"

The whole team is on the ice now and the adrenaline is running thick. Although all my guys are here with me, there's only one person I want to hug—only one person I want to kiss. I look up into the stands at Riley. She's standing and clapping. I point at her. She points back.

"We're going to celebrate so hard tonight," Marcus says.

With my eyes on the glowing light that is Riley, I nod. "Yes. Yes, we are."

***

Later that night, the team is at the bar. Everyone is cheering and celebrating, singing the celebration song. Everybody is in a good mood and the drinks are flowing. It's a rare moment of relaxation.

Looking down, I pull out my phone.

"Can you believe Edgar's pass?" Saito says, interrupting me. "That was *sick*."

"We need more of that for the playoffs," I say, shoving my phone back in my pocket.

Someone comes up behind me and pats me on the back with a strong hand.

"Guess who's probably winning the Corazon?" Marcus slams his mug of beer against mine, causing some to spill over.

"Let's not count our chickens before they hatch. That overtime goal gave me the exact same number of points that Coop has. At this point, it's all up to the journalists to determine the winner."

"Come on, at this point, it's practically guaranteed! What's more dramatic than winning a playoff position in overtime on the very last game of the regular season?"

He's right. Endorphins run through me. "God, I feel good. To the Blades!" I hold up a drink. Everyone follows my lead.

"To the Blades!"

We drink our beer. After a few more rounds of the celebration song, I finally find a quiet moment to pull out my phone to text Riley.

LOGAN: Are you around?

She reads the text but she doesn't respond right away. I stare at my phone way more than I mean to. Finally, she texts back.

RILEY: I'm at my room back on campus.

LOGAN: You should celebrate with us.

…typing…

RILEY: I'm just doing some last-minute work.

My heart sinks. It's completely like her to study late into the night. Still, I'm celebrating and it's been five days since I've seen her. All I want are her lips against mine.

LOGAN: Studying can wait until tomorrow. Tonight, we celebrate.

There's silence on her end. I'm wondering if I'm being too selfish. Maybe her silence all week was a sign.

But I felt how much she wanted me in the way she kissed me. I start typing again.

LOGAN: I want to see your eyes. And your body.

…typing…

RILEY: You're drunk.

LOGAN: Not yet. I can be if you want. You can take advantage of me.

RILEY: You wish.

I smirk.

LOGAN: And what if I do?

RILEY: Are you being serious right now?

LOGAN: Show up and find out.

A few minutes go by as I stare at the guys singing the celebration song again. When they get to the third verse, my phone lights up.

RILEY: Let me finish this cover letter and I'll see.

Smiling to myself, I slip my phone in my pocket. I want to keep sending her flirty texts but I know the faster she does her work, the faster she'll get out to the bar and be here with me.

The guys have another round of drinks. The singing turns into retellings of all our best plays of the game. When they're close to finishing their beers, I start getting nervous. I look at my phone. It's almost midnight.

Maybe Riley isn't coming after all.

Damn. Maybe she regrets that kiss the other day. I know I sure as hell don't.

"Hey, Logan…" A strange pink-haired woman in a low-cut red dress slips her hand across my leg. Her breath smells like garlic and whiskey. "I watched the game. You're such a stud out there."

I give her a tight smile. "Thanks."

"My name's Amanda."

Another hockey groupie.

"And yes, they're real," she says, bending over and flashing her cleavage at me. "If you want to touch them."

"No thanks," I say, looking back at the door.

The woman manages to wedge herself in front of me, forcing me to look at her. She puts her arms around my neck.

"I'll go down on you." Her pungent breath forces me to turn my head.

"Sorry, I have better things to do." I pull the woman's arms off my neck and pull away from her. I disappear into the crowd knowing that my six-foot-two stature won't make it easy. Hiding behind the other guys on the team, I check my phone again. It's been forty minutes since Riley's last text.

LOGAN: Are you coming?

I wonder if my text sounds too desperate but I send it anyway. Just as the text sends, the door to the bar opens and Riley steps in, looking like a light in a dark room. She's wearing form-fitting jeans and a pale pink silky spaghetti-strap blouse. She spots me across the room and smiles, filling my heart with warmth. Without hesitation, she walks straight over to me.

"I was starting to think you wouldn't show up," I say when she finally gets close.

"I heard a team won an important game or something." She smirks.

"Just a little bit important."

She leans in, bringing in the scent of green apple shampoo. *My summer goddess.*

"I wouldn't leave my boyfriend to celebrate alone, now would I?" She looks up with her gray sea-glass eyes.

"Boyfriend. I like that word." I push her wavy hair behind her ear. "God, you're gorgeous."

Her smile quickly disappears.

"We need to talk about something," she says.

"What is it?" I touch her waist.

She leans in again, lowering her voice. "The contract."

"Oh." I reclaim my hand. *Right. The contract.* "With how close we've been recently, it's easy to forget."

"That's what I want to talk about…"

I shake my head. “No.”

“No?”

“No talking tonight. Just celebrating…and dancing.” I grab her hand and pull her onto the dance floor. Pulling her close, I secure her hands on my chest as I put mine around her waist.

Her gray eyes look longingly up into mine.

“This is all I’ve been wanting all week,” I say.

She smiles. “I like seeing you in a good mood.”

“You put me in a good mood.”

She looks down and I can tell she’s blushing. As she looks back up with a smirk, her hands crawl up my chest and around the back of my neck.

I lean my forehead against hers as we dance. “I really like you, Riley Jamieson.”

She smiles.

“There’s something I really want to do right now,” I say in a low, rolling voice.

She looks me in the eyes. “Do it.”

That’s all the invitation I need. I lean in and press my lips against hers. She kisses me back, holding me close so I won’t pull away. The world around us fades away. Adrenaline and endorphins run through my veins and I know for certain that this is more thrilling than a last-minute overtime goal. She puts her hands in my hair as she deepens the kiss. I hold her tight, never letting go.

20

RILEY

Endorphins rush through my body. He deepens the kiss and I let out an involuntary moan as I melt against him.

What the hell am I doing?

A part of me is yelling, telling me to shut up and enjoy this. But I can't confuse my emotions like this. Jane was right about things getting messy. If he doesn't want to talk about the contract, does that mean the contract is still on? Is this kiss fake?

I pull back, breaking the kiss. I look into his eyes and it's enough to take my breath away. He's insanely handsome in his blue V-neck and dark jeans. He looks and smells so good that I almost can't resist pushing my paranoia aside and kissing him again.

Looking around, I notice the entire team is here, along with their wives and girlfriends. Lots of people have their phones out, whether they were filming us or not, I don't know.

This is definitely just for show.

The realization is sobering.

"Is everything okay?" He asks.

I look up into his dark lustful eyes.

"We should talk."

"What?" He yells over the music as he leans in. He presses his nose against my hair, lightly brushing the shell of my ear. I hear him inhale. *"I just want to dance with you."*

The bar cheers as members of the team make another toast.

"Logan! Get over here!" Someone calls out.

I feel Logan smile as he whispers in my ear. *"Hold on."*

He pulls away and joins the toast, leaving me to stand alone on the dance floor. I look around. Do I really fit in here? Is this all going to be over when the playoffs are over? So many questions that have no answers.

The song ends and another begins when I realize Logan is still celebrating with the guys.

"I'm just a prop," I mumble to myself. *"Don't forget that."*

Heart racing, I grab my purse and head outside for some fresh air. Rain is lightly sprinkling down over everything and the coolness of it refreshes my heated skin. Walking off the nerves calms me down a bit. I know I shouldn't be upset about a fake relationship, but I can't help the heat coursing through my chest. I close my eyes and breathe.

Swallowing past the lump in my throat, I look back at the bar where I can still hear the guys singing.

Breathe.

They erupt into cheers again.

My phone buzzes.

LOGAN: Where are you?

I almost don't want to respond, as if my tiny act of defiance might get under his skin.

LOGAN: Did you leave?

I ignore it and shove my phone in my purse. There. If he doesn't want to talk about the contract, we don't have to talk about anything at all. I continue walking, cursing myself for wearing heels. My phone buzzes against my thigh as I walk. He's calling me. I don't respond. The pressure in my chest is growing and pushing. I keep walking, hoping to just ignore it but the buzzing persists. I finally dig into my purse and pull my phone out. One missed call. Unable to hold in my feelings any longer, I text him. As I text, I press the screen so aggressively I feel like I'm popping bubble wrap.

RILEY: I'm going home.

LOGAN: Already?

I don't respond.

LOGAN: Are you okay?

RILEY: Clearly not.

LOGAN: Can we talk?

RILEY: You don't want to talk tonight, remember?

LOGAN: Riley, please...

He tries to call again but I ignore it. Tears are welling up in my eyes.

LOGAN: I'm an asshole for ignoring you.

RILEY: That's not it.

Exhaling sharply, I feel the pressure easing from my chest.

LOGAN: I know I'm a bit drunk, but I want you to know that I care about you. You're all I can think about right now.

RILEY: I thought that was the Corazon trophy.

I can see the three dots appearing and disappearing as he tries to find something to say. He doesn't respond for several minutes. I keep walking until I find a bus stop.

LOGAN: Please come to my place. I'll meet you there. Let's talk.

I stare at my screen. What the fuck am I going to do? Maybe it's best if I just go over and finish this. It'll be humiliating to break up with my fake boyfriend, but my emotions are too mixed up right now. I can't fake being his girlfriend after that kiss we shared in his kitchen. Continuing a fake relationship will just end in heartbreak.

Twenty minutes later I'm walking into the elevator and heading up to Logan's apartment. My heart is racing the entire trip over. When the doors open, I see him standing in the dim living room light. Shadows are cast over his face.

"I was hoping you'd show up," he says. "Come here."

I shake my head. "I want to know…what are we?"

"Riley…" He reaches for me.

The tension in my jaw is so tight I can feel the pressure in my teeth.

"No," I say. "I can't do that anymore. I can't be your fake girlfriend. I feel like there's *something* between us. Something more… and I can't show up to public events and prance around with you looking happy when I'm so confused. Is this real?" I look into his dark eyes.

He stays silent, staring at me. Those intense eyes of his refuse to look away. The tension grows until every molecule in the air between us is vibrating. I pull my gaze away and look down at my hands.

"I didn't want to talk about the contract," he says in a low voice, "because I was afraid this wasn't real and I didn't want you to end it."

Shocked, I look up at him. I can see the truth in his eyes.

Stepping closer, he takes my hands in his. "You're my best friend, Riley. And I wish I could show how important you are to me. It's *insane* how much I look forward to seeing you after a long day. I love coming home and seeing your stuff here. I love getting texts from you when I'm on the road. I love seeing you in the stands when I'm playing a game."

I can't help but smile.

"You're more than a contract to me, Riley."

I look up at him. His hand holds mine tighter as he steps closer.

"I don't want things to end between us, and I don't want you to think I'm using you. Your smile is the best part of my day."

My cheeks burn.

"This isn't about the trophy for me anymore." His dark eyes are staring deep into mine as if he can see my soul. I can smell his delicious masculine scent and the faint scent of beer on his breath. "No matter what happens, I want you to know that I like you. I really *really* like you." He squeezes my hands. "Tell me you feel the same way."

I smile. "I like you too, Logan Drake. You're my best friend. And I like you too much to fake it."

We smile at each other for a moment.

"Tell me this isn't just something you're saying after getting drunk."

He smiles. "I only had one drink."

"So," I say. "What do we do now?"

"Do you have the contract on you?"

Pulling my hands from his, I reach into my purse, find my wallet, and pull out the folded paper. "Here."

Logan takes it, unfolds it, and rips it into tiny little pieces.

"And just to make sure…" He brings it to the kitchen and drops it down the garbage disposal, pressing the button so that it chomps away at the little bits.

A surge of warmth rushes through my body and I smile as Logan walks back over to me.

"Now…where were we?" He steps closer and pulls me against him. He pushes my hair behind my ear and cups my face. He stares at me until the air is vibrating between us.

I hear his heartbeat in his breath.

He waits so long to make a move that I grow impatient and do it for him.

Pushing forward, I press my lips press against his. He kisses me back, deepening the kiss so that I can taste the beer on his lips. We kiss until we're breathing each other, inhaling each other. When I'm out of breath, I pull up and breathe the cool air, letting his lips find the curve of my neck. Our heavy breath drowns out the soft patter of rain on the windows.

"You don't know how long I've been wanting to do that," I whisper. Logan pulls back and looks into my eyes.

"What else have you've been wanting to do?" He asks. His voice is deep and dangerous, sending a shock straight to my core. The butterflies in my belly are fluttering like crazy.

"Everything," I whisper.

There's a hungry look in his eyes as he leans in and kisses me hard. There's no time for technique as our inhibitions disappear, letting our true feelings flow like water rushing out of a dam.

Lifting me with ease, he wraps my legs around his waist and carries me across the room, pressing my back against the wall. He pins his hips against me, holding me in place as he pulls off his shirt and tosses it aside. A whiff of his masculine aroma and sweat surrounds me. He places his hands on my waist, pulling off my silky blouse and dropping it on the ground. His hand moves up my bare belly and over my bra. Pulling the material down to expose my breast, he cups it with his warm hand.

"Logan," I moan.

He responds by kissing my neck, allowing his lips to explore my skin. His warmth surrounds me as I press myself against him. My hands move down his back and around front to his abs.

When I reach his belt, I unbuckle it and slide it free, letting it fall to the floor with a *thunk*. I unzip his pants which elicits a primal growl from deep in his throat. As if unable to stand it any longer, he lifts me again and carries me to the bedroom as we continue to kiss clumsily.

As he places me onto the bed, he stands over me, pulling off his pants. In the dim light, I can make out the silhouette of his body. He crawls onto the bed over me. Cool air blows in from the open window, chilling my skin. Logan lowers his head and his soft hair brushes my skin as he kisses the space between my breasts.

"We don't need this," he says as he unclasps my bra and tosses it aside. My nipples harden under the chilled air. I shiver under him.

"I'll keep you warm," he whispers. He pulls off boxer briefs and presses his naked body against me, bringing warmth and relief. "Is that better?"

"Yes," I whisper.

I don't have time to worry about timing or technique, or any of my insecurities that come with being so inexperienced. I'm too busy wanting Logan to place his lips anywhere and everywhere. I want to feel the smoothness of his lips on my skin. I want him to feel my heart pulsing as he places his mouth over my nipples.

Arching my body into his touch, I let him explore me. His hand moves over the top of my thigh and up over my silk underwear. His hand lingers, bringing warmth and pressure as he touches me. His fingers move softly and slowly, teasing me. I squirm under his touch, and under his gaze as he watches me with curious intensity. I bite my lip.

"Don't censor yourself." His deep voice whispers. *"I like hearing you moan."*

His hot breath blows over me and I let out an unrestrained whimper as I grab at the sheets.

"Logan—"

"Does this feel nice?"

"Yea—" I can't even say the full word before I'm pushing my head back into the pillow. "I want you to keep going. I want you—*inside*—"

He smirks before kissing his way down my body, slowly pulling my panties down over my thighs, allowing me to feel the silk fabric over every inch of my sensitive skin.

When he finally tosses them aside, he guides my legs apart and moves his hands slowly up my thighs.

"Why do you keep teasing me?" I ask.

"Because it's fun." He smirks.

I grab him and kiss him again, pulling him so that he's lying on top of me. I finally feel him for the first time as he presses hard against my thigh. I slowly move against him, teasing him just as he teased me.

He moans as he kisses my neck.

"Riley," he pleads in a quiet, strained voice. *"Please."*

I arch into his body as I wrap one leg around him.

"I've been dreaming of doing this with you," *I whisper.*

He looks down at me. His lust-filled eyes glow in the soft amber light coming in from the living room.

"I hope I live up to your expectations," he says, his body slowing pressing more pressure against mine.

In a moment, everything becomes frantic, fast, fulfilling. I gorge myself on the scent of him, that strong, intoxicating masculine scent. Moving my hands over his body, I explore the lines and shape of him, of the way he moves.

The lust, the desire is so overwhelming that I can't get enough. I ravage his mouth in an attempt to satiate myself but the need only becomes stronger, more ravenous.

His hands explore my body, my breasts as he presses his forehead against mine.

"Now," he says. *"Please."*

Thank god, I think to myself, because I need it now too.

As he drives into me, the pleasure shoots through my body, filling me with the dizzying feeling of stupefying satisfaction. I lose myself in the feeling. I lose myself in him. I hold onto Logan tight as our bodies move of their own volition, digging deeper and deeper. The bed creaks beneath us. Our frantic heavy breathing drowns out the drone of the pouring rain in the distance.

Logan clenches his body, his hands digging into my muscles as he shakes and triumphs. The world around us doesn't just shatter, it falls apart completely. Logan lets out a slow exhale as his heartbeat shakes his breath.

Drunk with the feeling, I lie limp under his weight. Tangled together with exhaustion and the suspended feeling of euphoria, neither of us moves as we catch our breath.

I kind of like it this way, feeling the pressure of his toned body on top of me, feeling his heart beating frantically against mine. Seeing him like this makes me feel like an absolute goddess.

When he finally lifts his head, we gaze into each other's eyes. I swear I can feel our bodies buzzing.

"I feel like I've just done drugs," I say.

He smirks. "I think we took that trip together."

He pushes a strand of hair out of my face.

"I thought we were going to break your bed at one point," I say.

He chuckles. "I'm surprised we didn't. That was several months of pent of sexual energy." He kisses my nose. "I think I need some water."

"Okay. Let's take a water break. Maybe get a snack. And we'll be ready to take that trip again in twenty minutes. Maybe we try to break the bed this time."

His weight strains against me as he gives me a deliciously devilish smile. "Fuck yes."

21

LOGAN

Riley and I spend all our free time in bed together before I have to leave with the team to prepare for the first playoff game of the season.

Holding her in my arms, I think about what we have. It's different. It's special. What we have together isn't just sex. It's mind-blowing sex. It's put-a-ring-on-it sex.

It's more than sex.

I listen to her gentle breathing, hoping that she doesn't have any regrets. She better not because I sure as hell don't. My only regret is not doing it sooner.

The alarm on my phone goes off.

"What's that?" She blinks a few times as she groggily sits up, looking around the room for the source of the noise.

"My alarm," I say. "I have to start getting ready. My flight is in a few hours."

"No," she protests, pouting her lips in the cutest way.

Smiling, I pull her close and kiss her on the forehead. "I'll be back soon, I promise."

I trace the bridge of her nose with the tip of mine before I climb out of bed and start to pack.

"Why don't you guys get more time off?" She's rubbing her eyes.

"Because people are excited about hockey. People like you."

"You know what else I'm excited for?" She looks at me with a lazy smile.

Looking at her, I smirk. I know exactly what she's implying. Throwing a t-shirt into my gym bag, I climb back onto the bed, crawling up her naked body.

"Trust me, I want to stay just as much as you do." I kiss her neck, unable to control the carnal growl deep in my throat as I smell her sweet scent.

She combs her fingers through my hair.

"Will you be at the home games when I'm back?" I ask.

"I'll try."

I pull back. "Free tickets to a playoff game and all you can do is try?"

She gives an apologetic shrug and pulls me close again. "I've got exams all week. There's a lot of studying to do."

"What will I do without my lady luck?"

Pulling her hand from my hair, she touches the rose pendant necklace hanging between her breasts. "If I could be there, I would. But I need to study."

"But you're so smart already, why do you need to study?"

She lets out a soft laugh.

"Here." Unclasping her necklace, she lifts my hand and drops the necklace into my palm. "That's where my luck comes from. Now it's yours."

"You don't need this for your exams?"

She shakes her head. "That's what studying is for. Take the necklace. That way I'm with you."

Smiling, I lean in and kiss her. "You're the best."

"Win those games."

"Am I in your playoff fantasy draft?"

She smirks. "Just win, okay?"

"Yes, boss." As I pull myself down her body, I kiss her thigh and blow a big raspberry against her skin before she shoves me off the bed.

***

The Blades fly out to play the first round against the Portland Wolves.

As I settle into my hotel room, I curse the sight of the large empty bed. It's hard not sleeping in the same bed as Riley after spending four days straight with her naked body pressed against mine. It's strange that I already miss her, despite only being gone now a few hours. I can't help but text her as I sit in the bus on the way to the arena. And I can't help but continually check my phone even though I know she's already too busy studying to respond. I can't help myself. She's the first woman I've ever felt this way about, and I don't want this relationship to slip through my fingers like smoke.

"Big game," Marcus says. We're standing in the locker room in the Portland arena. "Playoffs! We finally made it, bud."

"We sure did," I say.

I'm looking at my locker, hanging the rose pendant necklace in the perfect spot in the cubby so I can see it between periods.

"Damn," Marcus says. He's looking at his phone.

"What is it?"

"The Crushers are already leading."

"You know what?" I look at him. "I don't care. What matters is us. Right here, right now."

"Wow, you're in a good mood."

The rose pendant catches the light and I smile. "I feel more relaxed than I've felt in a long time, you know? I finally feel like I'm where I'm meant to be."

"Don't get too relaxed. We have a cup to win." Marcus throws the tape at me. I catch it with one hand. "Ready?"

"I was born ready."

After fifty-five minutes of playing a scoreless game, we manage to score by the skin of our teeth in the last five minutes thanks to a few lucky bounces.

The excitement of winning the first game of the playoffs is immense as the team celebrates.

After taking part in the post-game celebration, interviews, and team post-mortem, I shower and pack my things. Carefully taking the rose pendant out of my locker, I kiss it and put it securely in my bag. I can't help but feel like my good luck charm paid off.

There's a text message waiting for me.

RILEY: Nice assist ;)

I smile to myself.

LOGAN: You found time out of your busy schedule to watch me?

RILEY: How can I resist?

I'm about to send her a text about how much I miss her, how much I'm thinking about her, but she texts first.

RILEY: I can't stay up. Big study sesh tomorrow morning. Get some rest xox

LOGAN: Dream of me.

She sends back a smiley face. Smiling to myself, I pocket my phone and head to the hotel. Only forty-eight hours until I get to see her again.

God, what's wrong with me? How did I fall so hard for this woman? Not long ago, I was happy to be alone forever. Now I'm counting down the hours. The old me would think I was dumbstruck, an idiot. But Riley makes me feel complete. She makes my world feel full. Everything else seems secondary.

It's this exact attitude that loosens me up for the next game two days later. I pass the puck to everyone on my line, creating opportunities every time I'm on the ice. Our synergy allows Rory to score a hattrick while Skip gets a shutout.

Another win for the Blades. We're on fire!

I'm riding a high as I get back to Seattle that night and make my way home well past midnight. Something ignites inside me knowing Riley's there waiting for me.

I walk into a dark empty apartment.

"Riley?"

As I make my way into the bedroom, I see that the bathroom door is open. Steam is pouring out the door as the shower runs.

Smiling to myself, I put my bag down and start taking off my clothes. Taking off my watch, I place it on the dresser. One of the drawers is open and I can see her clothes neatly folded inside. A warm feeling radiates inside me knowing her stuff is mixed in with mine. It feels like she already lives here. Our lives are already intertwined.

For a moment, I envision what our living room would look like if all her stuff was here. I can even see us moving to a bigger place, one with an office and a backyard. A place we could call home.

A noise interrupts my fantasy.

Riley walks out of the bathroom wearing an oversized Blades t-shirt. A sleeve is hanging off her shoulder, showing off a pink bra strap. She's in black underwear. No pants.

"I didn't think you'd be back so soon." She dabs at her wet hair with a towel.

"I hurried because I was excited to see you." I take a step closer.

She throws the towel aside and walks up to me, placing her warm hands on my chest and bringing the clean smell of green apple shampoo and coconut body wash with her. She leans in, giving me a long, slow kiss. The exact one I've been waiting for. I close my eyes and lose myself in her lips. She tastes so good.

"Congratulations on your wins," she says.

"Thanks," I whisper. Leaning in, I kiss her again. "I missed you."

She smiles. "I missed you too."

This alone makes me feel at home.

"You know how my week was." I slip my hands around her waist. "How was yours?"

Her smile wavers and her chin quivers before she drops her face into her hands and begins to sob.

"Riley? What's wrong?"

She shakes her head.

"Hey, hey." I pull her hands from her face. "Look at me."

She looks up with her watery sea-glass eyes.

"What happened?"

Taking in a deep inhale, she pulls away and grabs a letter off the nightstand. She looks at it as she bites her lip as if debating if she should even show it to me.

"What is it?" I ask.

She hesitates before handing it to me. "The Seattle biomechanics lab decided not to take me on as an intern."

Her chin wrinkles.

"Oh, Riley." I set the letter aside. "Come here."

I pull her in so she can cry on my shoulder, which is exactly what she does.

'It's okay." I stroke her wet hair, inhaling the crisp scent of green apple.

"It's just not fair." She sobs softly as my shoulder starts to feel wet and warm. "I've worked so hard."

"You've got other internships or positions to apply to, right? I mean, this isn't the only one?"

She nods. "That's true, but…I just wanted to get this one."

She looks up at me with her watery eyes.

"Because of your Aunt Mary?" I ask.

Her mouth opens in astonishment. "You remember that?"

"Of course. It was on our first date at the charity gala. You said you wanted to work at the biomechanics lab here in Seattle because you wanted your Aunt Mary to be proud of you."

She sniffles. "I can't believe you remember that!"

"It was important to you." I touch her wet cheek. "I think your Aunt Mary will be proud of you no matter where you end up. You're a smart independent woman who can get any position she wants. It doesn't have to be at the same place she worked at. There's no way she's not proud of you already."

"You think so?"

"I *know* so. You know how I know?"

She shakes her head.

"Because I'm proud of you." I wipe away her tears. "You're determined and smart, and that's a deadly combination."

She laughs but her smile quickly fades. "I just had my heart set on a job here in Seattle for so long…"

I furrow my brow. "You don't have any other prospects here?"

She looks up at me and quickly looks away. "I still have one place I'm waiting to hear back from but if it falls through then I'll have no choice but to move."

There's a vulnerability in her voice that makes my stomach twist. This was supposed to be just the beginning of our relationship, not the end. It makes me want to fix everything so that we can be together, the way we are in my fleeting fantasies.

I look into her eyes. "Everything will be okay. I believe in you, Riley Jamieson."

She smiles. "Thanks, Logan Drake."

"I can see you living here, with me," I say. My heart is thumping in my chest.

"You can?"

I nod as I tilt her chin up and kiss her. My lips brush against hers slowly, passionately. She places her hands on my chest, moving them slowly up to my shoulders. I clasp my hand over one of hers.

"I love you," I whisper against her lips.

I feel her smile. Her trusting gray sea-glass eyes look up into mine.

"I love you too."

I don't know what else to do but smile.

"That's the first time we've ever said that," she says.

"But I know you've loved me all along."

She furrows her brow and laughs. "What?"

"You told me on our date at the student bar that the next person you had sex with would be the man you loved."

Her cheeks turn pink. She looks down, trying to hide her smile. I tilt her chin back up so she can look at me. I wrap my arms around her, pulling her body against mine, feeling her softness and heat. She trails her hands down my back, slipping her fingers under the waistband of my jeans.

"Come on, Mr. Drake." She tugs at my jeans, pulling my hips against hers. "Show me how much you love me."

She pulls me down onto the bed with her.

"I can do that." I smirk as I pull her oversized Blades shirt off, revealing the pink lace bra and mismatched black cotton panties underneath.

I kiss her shoulder, inhaling her as if she might disappear soon. She runs her hands through my hair, breathing in my ear. We paw at each other like hungry wolves, starved for each other's affection.

The relief of connection is more intense and invigorating than anything felt before. We move against each other slow and steady like ocean waves, rolling together in the still of the night, becoming one with the rhythm.

I stare into those gray sea-glass eyes, feeling the hope I feel for both of us. Wanting to become one with her, I press my lips against hers, kissing her with the knowledge that she's all I'll ever need.

"Please," she moans. "Let's do this all night."

I kiss her neck and breathe into her ear. "Let's do this forever."

22

RILEY

Balancing school and my social life, I manage to schedule the insane amount of studying I have to do around Logan's hockey schedule. It's impossible not to drop work to go to the games, especially when Logan always gets me amazing seats.

And besides, the studying and the hockey distract me from the fact that I lied to Logan. I told him I had another prospect here in Seattle which wasn't true. I still have a chance for positions in Chicago and New York, but none from Seattle. That ship has sailed.

I lied to Logan. *I lied to Logan.*

Why did I lie to Logan?

A nervous feeling comes over me.

I can still see Logan's hopeful face, gleeful at the thought of me staying here with him. And the thought is just as tempting for me. Living with Logan would be an absolute dream. But what would that mean for us? Would this be a long-term thing? For the moment, I'm still in shock that we said the L-word to each other.

Choosing to focus on the good, I go to that night's game straight after a six-hour study session. As the game starts, the energy in the arena is absolutely electric. The crowd is on fire, the players even more so. This is the best the Blades have played all season and all eyes are on one player.

Logan has had a phenomenal run so far and every time he scores, he looks right at me and points. It's thrilling knowing that when millions of people are looking at him, he's looking at me.

The Blades win both home games, easily sweeping the Wolves in the first round.

Between my study groups and his practice sessions, we spend as much naked time together as we can before he has to leave again.

"Don't leave," I say.

He's sitting on the bed wearing nothing but his underwear. I'm sitting on his lap, nuzzling my nose against his neck. He smells like fresh pine and aftershave. His strong arms wrap around me as he softly kisses my cheek.

"I'll sweep the next team too," he says with a low growl in his voice which stirs me deep inside. "I'll have more time with you."

"Mmm." I smile. "I like that plan."

We say goodbye longer than any sane couple should before he finally gets dressed and heads to the airport again. He'll be in Sacramento for the next four days as the Blades play the first two games against the Skates.

When the elevator doors close and the apartment is completely silent, I instantly feel guilt churning in my belly.

Although I have over thirty physics chapters to review, I spend most of my morning searching for job opportunities in Seattle with no luck. Every link is already purple, meaning I've clicked on the posting already once before. There's nothing new, nothing relevant to my specialties.

I instinctively touch my necklace for some good luck, but it's not there. I feel naked.

Anxiety starts creeping in. I can't stop thinking about Logan and our relationship. I want it to continue *so badly* and see where this goes. But how can that happen if I leave?

There's no way he'd move for me… right?

After all, he just moved here. Why would he want to move again?

I sigh and deflate in my seat. I force myself to forget all this and focus on studying. If I don't pass these exams, I won't be eligible for any jobs *anywhere.*

On the second day that Logan's gone, the wind picks up in the city, rattling the windows of the empty apartment. The sky is dark and gray but Logan's apartment feels cozy with its warm lights and an endless supply of artisan tea. Logan's healthy habits are slowly rubbing off on me.

Only a few hours until the game. I have plans later to watch it with Madeline and Jane. Madeline was insistent on hosting as she bought the cable sports package solely to watch Logan. She was so excited that I couldn't say no. And it doesn't help that Jane made fast friends with Madeline when I introduced them a few weeks ago. Jane wanted to see Logan's apartment and I ran out of excuses for saying no.

As I force myself to focus on my studies, I realize I forgot my mechanical physics textbook in my dorm room and I'll have to pick it up before the game starts. I check the time, realizing there's not much left. Pulling on my jeans, a Blades t-shirt, and a black windbreaker, I head to campus.

As I ride the light rail train to the university station, I notice the city is buzzing with excitement for the game. Even though the Blades are in another state, a lot of people are wearing their Blades shirts and jerseys.

I smile to myself, proud of Logan and the rest of the guys. Checking my phone, I see that I've still got enough time to get my book and make my way back to Madeline's in time for the puck-drop.

Hurrying across campus, I feel big fat drops of rain coming down. Picking up my pace, I manage to get inside right before it really starts pouring.

As I walk by the student lounge, a nasal voice calls out.

"Who's this stranger?" The voice asks.

Standing in the doorway of the student lounge, I look inside. There's only one person in there.

"Oh, hi Keith," I say unenthusiastically.

He's sitting on the couch with his sneakers on the coffee table. There are several pieces of paper scattered over the table along with an open can of cheap beer. I recognize the beer as the one that's been in the communal fridge since last Halloween.

The TV is on the sports network. Two sportscasters are discussing the stats between the Blades and the Skates. Pre-game coverage has already begun.

"Hey," Keith says. "Have you found a job yet?"

I pull my eyes from the TV. "I have some prospects. You?"

He uses his chin to point at the papers on the table. "I've written a hundred cover letters. If I don't get anything I'm fucked."

"Any frontrunners?"

"Not really. I thought I had an interview in the bag last week, but that job went to Cassidy Simons. Suck-up. All the good jobs are being taken by the brown-nosers."

I raise my eyebrow. "Seriously? Those people got jobs because they're freaking smart and got good grades."

"Yeah, whatever. If I don't find anything by the end of the month then I'll be out on my ass."

"Unless your parents let you stay in their basement."

"Ha-ha," he says sarcastically. "They're not letting me do that again."

Tired of the conversation, I look back at the TV screen where they're discussing Logan. The image cuts to him skating across the ice.

"They're already warming up? What time is it?" My heart picks up its pace as I realize I need to get going.

"Six-thirty," Keith says, looking at me with a mischievous twinkle in his eye. "Your boyfriend's out of town, huh?"

I give him a sharp stare. "Don't even think about it."

Unimpressed, Keith looks back down at the table. "I need food. I'm heating up some ramen. Want some?"

"Ramen?" I wrinkle my nose. "Seriously?"

"I'm broke, give me a break. Not all of us have the privilege of dating a multi-millionaire," he scoffs as he gets up and stumbles out of the room.

My eyes dart back to the TV screen. The guys file off the ice.

"Alright folks, twenty minutes until the anthem. We'll discuss our predictions after these messages."

Shit.

If it's still raining, I'm going to be late getting to Madeline's. As I pull my phone out to text Jane, it starts ringing. It's Logan.

"Hello?"

"Hey," Logan says.

He's out of breath.

"Aren't you about to play?" I ask. "I just saw you on the ice."

"Yeah, I'm just calling to see how studying is going."

I smile. Even when he's about to play one of the most important games of his career, he's thinking about me.

"It's going pretty good. I'm about to take a break to watch you."

"Oh good," Keith says loudly as he barges back into the room with his plastic bowl of ramen. "You didn't take my place."

He drops onto the couch, nearly spilling his ramen all over himself.

"Who's that?" Logan asks.

"Just Keith. I'm on campus picking up a book."

"Oh, you're so hot and spicy," Keith moans as he slurps up some noodles.

"Huh?" Logan asks.

"He's talking about his twenty-cent ramen," I say as I watch Keith eat with the dexterity of a toddler. "Ugh."

I head out into the hallway for some privacy.

"Good luck tonight. I'll be watching with Madeline and Jane."

"You better get there quick. I'm planning on putting on a show for you."

I smirk. God, even his voice is sexy.

"Oh, by the way. Management wants to have a big dinner after the second round is over. It's Coach's birthday. Would you be down to be my date?"

"Of course." I bite my lip. "Do you even have to ask?"

"I don't want to interfere with your studies."

"I think I can make time to spend a night with Logan Drake in a suit."

"Great." I can hear the smile in his voice. "There's gonna be a lot of journalists there so this will be a good way to campaign for the Corazon."

My smile disappears. For a moment I'm stunned.

"Oh…right." I hadn't thought about the Corazon or that Logan was still campaigning for it. Lightning cracks outside, lighting the inside of the hallway. "Listen, good luck tonight. I need to get going if I want to watch you play."

"Alright. I love you."

I hesitate for a moment.

"I love you too. Bye."

I shove my phone into the pocket of my windbreaker. My heart is thumping in my chest. Anxiety twists in my belly. Why is he talking about campaigning for the Corazon? I thought I was no longer a prop for that.

"Fifteen minutes until the big game!" The sportscaster announces from the TV in the other room.

Crap. If I leave now, I might get to Madeline's in time.

As I'm about to leave, I realize I still haven't picked up my book. As I walk back past the student lounge, Keith's curious eyes watch me. There's a big shit-eating grin on his face.

"What?" I ask.

"You guys love each other? That's a big step."

"You were listening to us? Maybe you should mind your own business."

He shrugs. "It's just that a guy like him and a nerdy student like you doesn't really make sense to me, you know?"

My blood runs cold. "What do you mean by that?"

"A millionaire hockey player doesn't usually fall for someone who's a seven on a good day. Athletes date tens. Even the ugly athletes date tens."

"Ugh, you're disgusting. Thanks for reminding me why I never talk to you."

"Hey, we don't have to talk to have a good time!" He smirks.

I roll my eyes. "If I'm a seven and I'm out of your league, what does that make you?"

"Hey, I'm an equal opportunist. When you two break up, you'll know where to find me."

"Your parents' basement?" I clap back.

He looks at me with a dumbfounded look as I pull away. Making my way to my room, I get my book and rush off campus back to the light rail station.

Damp from the rain, I sit on the train and make my way to Madeline's apartment. As I stare out the window, an unsettling feeling pools in my belly as my thoughts spiral.

Maybe Keith is right. Maybe Logan is planning to break up with me soon. Maybe our entire relationship really is about the Corazon trophy after all.

Before I know it, I'm sitting in Madeline's living room. Jane and I are sitting on the black vinyl couch while Madeline sits on a pink feather lounge chair. Ravioli, her cat, is stretching on a silky red love-seat in the corner.

We're sipping chamomile tea from gold-plated teacups while a washed-up singer belts the American anthem on the high-definition TV. The smell of lemon biscuits wafts from the kitchen.

I stay uncharacteristically silent as I watch the camera panning over the team as they stand on the ice, waiting for the game to start.

The game cuts to a commercial break.

Jane uses the time to explain to Madeline how to identify a man with a perfect ass.

"It has to be round and perky if that makes sense." Jane mimes a squeezing motion with her hands.

"Trust me." Madeline's sharp eyes glimmer behind her bifocals. "I've seen my share of perfect behinds."

"Ooh!" Jane's eyes grow wide as she leans in. "*Do* tell."

"You girls!" I say. "Are you sure you're not teenagers?"

They both giggle.

The game comes back on.

"Should we bet that Logan scores before the end of the period?" Madeline smiles devilishly.

"Oh, no," I say. "I can't jinx my boyfriend like that!"

Jane laughs into her teacup. "Yeah right. Logan is such an overachiever he'll probably get a hattrick before the end of the period. At this rate, he's a lock for the Corazon."

Of course, he is.

I clench my jaw and my thoughts spiral as I think about Logan's words from earlier.

My phone buzzes. I expect to see Logan's name, which is completely silly since he's on the ice right now.

The call is from an unknown number.

I excuse myself and take the call in the kitchen.

"Hello?"

"Hello, is this Riley Jamieson?"

"Yes…"

"This is Clara Fitzpatrick from the Biomech Research Solutions Lab in New York City. We received your application and we're very impressed."

"Oh wow, thank you!" My heart starts thumping harder in my chest.

"We'd like to offer you the opportunity to fly out here for an interview and a tour of the facilities. Please keep in mind that we have about thirty other interviewees so this will be a very cutthroat process."

"I understand."

"If you are interested, please respond before the weekend as we'd like to start flying out interviewees by next week."

"Of course. Thank you so much."

I end the call with shaky hands.

"Oh my god, oh my god!"

I walk out into the living room where both Jane and Madeline are looking up at me.

"What is it?" Madeline asks in her old creaky voice.

"The research center in New York City wants to interview me!"

Jane jumps to her feet. "Oh, Riley, that's fantastic!"

I'm biting my lip.

Her smile disappears. "Wait, why aren't you more excited?"

"It's Logan, isn't it?" Madeline asks.

I nod as I drop myself back onto the couch and bring my hands to my face. "Oh, this is so stupid. I wasn't supposed to get this attached. I wasn't supposed to fall for him!"

"Aww," Jane and Madeline moan in unison.

"That's not helping." I exhale sharply. "What am I supposed to do?"

"Do you love him?" Madeline asks.

I hesitate as I stare at the screen where the guys are skating across the ice. "I don't even know what love is."

"Nobody does." Madeline leans on her frail arm. "That's what makes it so messy. What I know is that you two care for each other. I see it in the way you two giggle when you go up the elevator, and the way Logan talks about you."

I smile.

"Follow your gut," the old woman continues. "That's all you can do." She leans over and squeezes my knee.

"Sure…my gut, because that'll be easy. What if my gut doesn't tell me anything?"

"It will. It always does." She winks at me in a way that makes me feel like she just sprinkled fairy dust in the air.

The timer goes off in the kitchen.

"The lemon biscuits!" She says happily.

"Let me help," Jane says.

"Hogwash!" Madeline waves her away. "I need the exercise."

It takes her a full thirty seconds to push her creaking bones into an upright position. When she finally makes it to her feet, she shuffles slowly to the kitchen. After lazily watching the scene unfold, Ravioli gets up, stretches, yawns, and jumps onto the floor, following jauntily behind her.

When they make it into the kitchen, I turn to Jane.

"What should I do?" I ask.

"What do you want to do?"

I sigh. "I think I have something really special here with Logan, but at the same time, this is my career we're talking about. I don't have any other options!"

"What does your gut say?" She asks.

"It's telling me I want both Logan and the fancy career. But I don't think life works that way."

"Would he be down for a long-distance thing?"

"I don't know, I don't know." I push my hair back. "Ugh, I'm just so confused about everything."

"Riley." She gives me that look like she can see right through me. "Tell me what's wrong."

I look up into her eyes. "He referenced the Corazon trophy today."

"So?"

"Our contract was put in place for him to clean up his reputation enough to win that trophy. He invited me to some party this weekend and told me it'd be good for his trophy prospects."

I sigh as I bury my face in my hands. My skin is hot.

"I don't know why he said that," I say. My hands muffle my voice. "The contract is over. We ripped it up."

"Maybe he's worried," Jane says.

"Why?"

"Well…have you guys gone out in public together since ending the contract?"

I think for a moment. "Well, I've been to games but we haven't been to any events together."

"Maybe he's nervous about that."

"He really shouldn't be. I mean, we're amazing together at home."

"And he can still try to win the trophy, right?" Jane asked sincerely. "He has career goals just like you do."

I sigh and nod. "You're right. I shouldn't read too much into this."

"Are you gonna be okay?" Jane squeezes my arm.

I nod and give her a close-lipped smile. My stomach feels a little bit more settled but the whole moving thing is still on my mind. I'll have to call the research center in New York City before the end of the week to schedule the interview.

The TV casts a harsh white light onto the living room as the camera pans over the ice. The referee drops the puck and the Blades gain possession of it almost instantly.

As I watch number thirteen skate around the ice, I think about what a long-distance relationship would be like. I already spend so much time away from Logan that I can't imagine moving all the way to the opposite coast and seeing him even less than I do now.

"And here's a breakaway for Logan Drake—he shoots he scores! Holy moly! The nerve of this kid!"

Jane cheers and I manage to snap out of my mental spiral to cheer with her. We watch as Logan celebrates with the other players.

"Did I miss it? Did I miss it?" Madeline shuffles into the living room faster than I've ever seen her move. Her frail blue-veined hands are clutching a plate of lemon biscuits.

"Logan scored!"

"Yes!" Madeline does a cute little bounce in celebration. "Lemon biscuits and a goal by Logan Drake. How can life be any better?"

Yeah, I think to myself as I watch Logan skate past his team's bench, fist-bumping each teammate along the way. *How can life be any better?*

23

LOGAN

After another two wins in Sacramento, I come back to an empty apartment in Seattle. With Riley's intensely long study sessions at the library and my busy playoff schedule, we barely get to see each other.

When the Blades meet the Skates during game three, I see Riley in the crowd. Her presence gives me enough energy to set up two goals, gaining me two assists and getting the Blades another win.

She's so busy at school that I don't even get to thank her for bringing me good luck before the Blades are back in the arena for game four.

This time, she's not in the crowd.

This throws me off my game as I mishandle two passes and slip up on what could have been a game-tying goal. It's the first loss for the Blades since the playoffs started, meaning we'll have to go back to Sacramento.

Although the Blades still have the lead, the trip means less time with Riley.

We cross paths the next morning in my apartment before I head to the airport again.

She's standing in the kitchen pouring herself a mug of coffee. She's already dressed, looking like she's about to head out soon.

"You weren't at the game last night," I say.

"I'm sorry." She holds the mug in both hands and sips. "I had a late study group that went until two in the morning. It was brutal."

She puts down the mug. "I saw you had a bad night too."

"It wasn't my best." I walk over to her and pull her into my arms as I push a strand of hair behind her ear. "I missed you."

She smiles. "I missed you too."

I kiss her neck, smelling the vanilla perfume on her jawline.

"I can't stay." She pushes me away. "I have to get to campus."

"So soon?" My stomach sinks. "I won't be back for another few days."

"Win the next one and you'll be here sooner." She smirks.

"You know how to motivate me." I pull her back close to me and kiss her lips slowly, enjoying each second.

She kisses me back before slowly pulling away. "I have to go."

"Is everything alright?" I hold her dainty hand in mine.

"Yeah, I'm just really busy. I'm sorry." She pulls back.

"I'll see you in a few days."

She smiles. "I'll see you on TV."

Grabbing her bag, she makes her way to the elevator. As she disappears inside and the doors slide shut, I'm left alone in my kitchen.

There was something strange about her behavior.

I pick up her mug and take a sip. She didn't even finish her coffee.

Walking back to my room, I pass the dining room table which is littered with papers. A letter is sitting on top. It's from a place in New York City.

I pick it up and read it.

"They're sending her a plane ticket to go in for an interview?" I mumble to myself. "Why didn't she tell me about this?"

Is this why she's acting so strange? Is she taking a job in New York City and she's afraid to tell me?

I find myself staring at the letter long enough for the coffee to start going cold. I'm lost in my thoughts as I entertain every possibility.

Is Riley being distant because she knows she'll have to leave soon? Is this her way of avoiding becoming attached?

I look around my apartment: the notebooks and pens on the coffee table, the shoes by the entrance, the hair clips everywhere.

My gut wrenches.

I don't want Riley to leave. I like having her presence around. If she moves, this will be the same lifeless apartment it's been since the beginning. The thought of it sends chills through me.

I can't even imagine a life without Riley.

The alarm on my watch goes off.

Shit.

I spend two minutes throwing clean clothes into a bag before driving myself to the airport.

I spend the plane ride with my headphones on and the rose pendant in my hands. I want to fight to be with Riley, but how? I can't force her to stay in Seattle if she gets a job in New York City.

Coach walks down the airplane aisle, heading to the washroom.

"Drake!" He speaks forcefully enough for me to hear it through my headphones. I pull them off.

"Yes, Coach?"

"You getting your head in the game this time?"

"Of course, Coach."

"Good. I was just talking to Balder and he's worried about you."

I'm staring at Coach but I'm thinking about Riley.

"Balder?" I ask absently.

"Good god, kid. Take a nap if you're tired. We don't need more mistakes."

"Yes, sir."

Coach continues down the aisle as I stare at the seat-back in front of me.

Looking down, I inspect the rose pendant necklace in my hand. Suddenly, an idea pops into my head. I know exactly what I need to do.

***

After a win on the road to secure the team's advancement to the third round, the Blades head back home. Depending on the winner of the other matchup, the

Blades might be playing against the Crushers in the semi-finals.

As the team takes their much-deserved break, everyone looks forward to celebrating Coach's birthday. Meanwhile, I look forward to seeing Riley.

With all these road trips and games, I've barely spent ten minutes with Riley in the past week. Text messages between us have been few and far between making us feel even further apart. I don't like it.

When I'm finally home, I shower and change into a crisp dark blue suit. After adjusting my black skinny tie in the mirror, I reach into my bag and pull out a small box. Opening it, I admire the diamond ring, custom made with the same rose design as Riley's grandmother's pendant. I had enough time in San Francisco to get it custom made.

Closing the box, I place it in my pocket. Looking in the mirror, I make sure the bulge doesn't stick out too much. I'll have to keep it secret until I find the perfect moment, sometime when we're alone and the mood is just right. This way she'll know I'll follow her wherever she goes, that I'm committed to her.

The door bursts open and Riley pushes her way in. I instinctively touch my pocket before crossing my arms, trying to look casual.

"I'm sorry I'm late," she says. Her messy bun is completely disheveled and she's carrying more books than she looks comfortable carrying. She drops them onto the bed before pulling her hair-tie off, shaking out her wild hair. "I'll be ready in fifteen."

She gives me a quick kiss before rushing into the master bathroom and shutting the door. I don't even have a chance to say hello.

I know she's been busy and a part of me wants to tell her to take the night off and study but I can't wait any longer. I miss her. I miss the way she smells. I miss the way she feels in my arms, especially when she rests her head against my chest and I get to smell the intoxicating scent of her apple shampoo and vanilla perfume. I want those moments for the rest of my life.

The sound of the shower is followed by the sound of a hairdryer. Ten minutes later, Riley walks out in a white cocktail dress that hugs all her curves just right. Her hair is styled into waves and she's all glammed up.

I smile goofily as I stare at her.

"You look beautiful," I say.

She smirks as she walks up to me. "You clean up pretty nicely yourself, Mr. Drake."

She places her hands on my chest. The green apple aroma fills the space between us and I instantly feel like jelly in her hands.

"I missed you," I say with a low growl.

Her gray sea-glass eyes look up into mine. "I missed you too."

Pushing in, I press my lips against hers. It's a kiss that I've been dreaming about for days and it rattles my bones just like I thought it would.

"Are you ready for a night of debauchery?" I ask as I press my forehead against hers.

"Ooh, is that what tonight is?"

"It could be." I kiss her again.

"In that case, yes," she says in a low, seductive voice. "I'm totally ready."

"There's nothing sexier than the word yes," I say in a low growl as I place my hands on her curves. "Can't we just stay here?" I moan.

She smiles. "We can do whatever we want."

Her hands caress the back of my neck.

"Riley Jamieson, don't tease me like that." I kiss her again.

"But it's so fun," she whispers. Her breath feels warm against my neck.

Her hands get adventurous and move down my belly. She's just about to touch my pants and feel what's in my pocket when I pull back.

"Come on," I say, trying to hide how abrupt I just acted. "We should go if we want the good appetizers."

I have no interest in pulling away from her, especially when she smells and looks like *that*, but I can't spoil the secret. Not yet. Tonight is going to be a night to remember and I have to keep my cool.

During the car ride, I share stories about the game in Sacramento. Riley stays awfully quiet and I think I know why.

When we arrive at the restaurant, the clouds are rolling in. We make our way inside where the celebration dinner is taking place.

As usual, Blades management has spared no expense. The party has delicious appetizers, tall glasses of champagne, and live jazz. The media is there asking questions with oversized microphones as flashbulbs go off all around us.

I look around at the hundreds of blurry faces. My forehead feels heated. I can feel the ring box in my pocket pressing against my thigh.

Riley looks at me with big gray eyes.

I take her dainty hand in mine.

"Are you okay?" She squeezes my hand.

Wanting to keep her from becoming suspicious, I give her an abrupt nod. "There's a lot of people here tonight… including the voting committee for the Corazon."

Her smile disappears. My palms are getting damp.

"Where's the bar?" She asks, looking around. "I need a drink."

"Hey." I pull her back. "Let's dance first."

Riley looks around uncomfortably. "Okay."

I pull her onto the dance floor and place my hand on her waist as we dance to slow jazz.

"I missed you," I say.

She smiles. "I'm right here."

I hold her close and take a deep breath.

"Yes," I whisper. "I've got you."

She smirks. "What are you gonna do about it?"

I take a deep breath. "I want you to know that no matter what happens over the next few weeks, I'll be there to support you. And I'll be by your side every step of the way."

"Logan—" Riley looks away.

Her tone feels like a cold hand gripping my heart.

"I think I know what you're about to say," I say.

"No," she says. She takes a deep breath and looks into my eyes. "I need to know if this is real."

I furrow my brow. "What do you mean?"

"You said something the other night, and again tonight, that makes me think the contract isn't over—"

"Oh."

Confusion reigns as other couples dance around us.

"What did I say?"

She swallows. "That it would look good for your Corazon award campaign if I was here with you."

"Did I say that?"

"Yes!"

"Riley, I didn't mean it that way. I just meant that—" I can't find an explanation in time and it's enough to incriminate me. Her eyebrows knit together.

"Is this all for show?" Tears start welling up in her eyes. "Am I just a piece of PR jewelry for you?"

"No, of course not." This night is going south fast. "I didn't bring you here for that."

She pulls away from me and walks off the dance floor. I follow her to a quiet corner of the restaurant.

When she turns around, her face is red and her arms are crossed.

"Do you know how much it hurts?" She asks. "To commit yourself to someone only to hear that you're only there for show?"

"Riley, I wasn't thinking. We both know I'm not the smart one in this relationship."

She doesn't smile. Instead, she exhales sharply and looks away, her jaw clenched.

"This relationship," she repeats. "What exactly *is* this relationship?"

"It's real." I take her hands in mine. "And I want to be with you. No matter what happens in our future, I want to be with you." I look into her eyes. "This is real, *I swear.*"

"Then why doesn't it feel that way?" Her big gray eyes look up at me as her chin wrinkles. Tears begin crawling down her face. She turns away.

"Riley—" My phone buzzes in my pocket. I ignore it. "Riley, please—"

I reach for her but she pulls away.

"I just need a moment to breathe." She walks to the exit and out into the parking lot.

I exhale in exasperation. As I follow her, my phone continues buzzing. I pull it out and check the screen. There's a text from an unknown number.

UNKNOWN NUMBER: Send me one million dollars or this pic goes viral.

"What the—"

I check the attached picture. My body goes cold when I see a snapshot of the contract, completely intact as if it had never been ripped.

"What the fuck?"

My heart is racing and heat rises to my face. I look up and run outside and across the parking lot after Riley.

"Riley!" I call out as I catch up to her.

She looks up, her eyes are red and her makeup is smeared from crying.

"What?" She asks.

"What is this?" I ask.

She instantly looks confused.

My hands are shaking as I hold the phone up, showing her the message.

She looks at the screen as her eyes grow wide. "What the hell?"

She looks up at me. I shake my head.

"You really think I'd do this?" She asks.

"Well, you had the contract the whole time. It was in your possession. You're the only person who could have taken this picture."

Riley is staring at me in a way I've never seen before. "Do you really think I'd sabotage my reputation to destroy yours? Do you really think I'd want to destroy yours at all?"

"You're telling me you didn't tell a single soul about this contract?"

"Of course not!"

"Not even Jane?"

She opens her mouth but closes it without saying anything. The guilt in her eyes tells me everything I need to know.

My heart sinks. "You did, didn't you?"

"Jane wouldn't tell anyone," she says. "I *swear*. She was the one who told me about the app to begin with! If it weren't for her, I would have never met you. There's no reason she'd blackmail us. I had to speak to her about this because I didn't know—"

"Didn't know what?" I keep my gaze locked on her. Rage is starting to bubble up inside me.

"I didn't know if this was real." She looks at me. "Is it real? You're still talking about impressing everybody so that you can win the Corazon. Behind closed doors, everything makes sense, but out here *nothing* makes sense. So please tell me because it's driving me crazy. Is this real?"

I stare into those big sad eyes.

My first instinct is to tell her this is real, that I'd marry her if it meant keeping her hand in mine. But the annoyance of betrayal bubbles through me.

My silence lasts a little too long. I pull my gaze away.

"Look at me, Logan." Her voice is shaking.

My gaze darts everywhere but her. Finally, I force myself to look at her. My heart is buzzing in my chest. Riley is clenching her jaw tight. Tears glisten in her eyes.

"Real couples are supposed to trust each other," I say.

"*I didn't do it.* And neither did Jane. I *promise* you."

"You had *one* secret to keep for me. One. And you couldn't even do that." My voice is shaking. "I can't believe this is happening."

"There's no way she would have done this!"

"How can you be so sure?" I ask scathingly. I can hear how angry I'm getting. I look away and force myself to breathe.

Music is pouring out of the restaurant as the door is propped open by bystanders. People are starting to gather and watch us as we argue in the parking lot. Some of them even have their phones out. *Crap.*

"We're making a scene," I say.

Riley shakes her head. "That's all you ever care about, isn't it? You just want people to think you're some amazing guy. But in reality, you're such a fucking coward."

"Riley—"

"You're too afraid of real relationships so you push everyone away. You lost Harrison Cooper, you lost the Crushers, and now you've lost me." Tears roll down her cheeks. "I'm stupid for believing this was real, and for believing that a guy like you could have loved someone like me."

She pulls away. Feeling defeated, I let her leave.

Looking back, I see the crowd is still standing near the door. Allowing some time for my nerves to calm, I stay outside. The cool breeze relieves my heated skin.

My life unraveled in five short minutes. I can't go back inside. Being at a party alone after a public breakup is not a good look. And there's a text on my phone threatening to end my career.

Why did she tell Jane?

Who else would it be? They were the only people who knew about the contract. Was this a long-con? A way to get money for the two of them?

Riley couldn't be the one to do this to me, right? Or maybe I was wrong this whole time. Maybe she's just like the other women who've screwed me over in the past.

I sigh as I start walking to my car.

I told myself not to trust anyone. I told myself not to put down my defenses. And this is where it led me.

As I walk, I feel my phone buzzing against the ring box in my pocket.

24

RILEY

What an asshole.

Tears stream down my face as I make my way back to the university campus as fast as I humanly can.

I'm such a goddamn fool.

I catch a bus and find an isolated seat in the back. I pull out my phone, half expecting to see a text or a missed call from Logan. Instead, I see notifications about our very public breakup. I turn off my phone and shove it in my purse.

How could he blame me for all this? Didn't he trust me?

The rejection. The humiliation. I hide my face when I get to campus but that doesn't stop the whispers and the stares.

I don't care. The pain is pulsing in my chest like the aftermath of a bomb that just exploded. Everything inside me is empty. My heart is gone.

Making my way up to my room, I push the door open to see Jane on her bed listening to ethereal music and reading a magazine. She looks up and instantly reacts to my disheveled state.

"Riley." She tosses the magazine aside. "Are you okay?"

She rushes over to me.

I shake my head as the tears start streaming again.

"Oh my god, what's wrong?"

"The contract," I say between sobs. "Did you take a picture of it?"

"What?" Her face contorts in confusion. "What are you talking about?"

Through heavy sobs, I explain everything to her – the text, the accusations from Logan, the breakup.

She shakes her head. "No, I didn't have anything to do with that. I didn't even see the contract!"

It's true. I kept it in my wallet from the moment we signed it and it stayed there until Logan and I ripped it up.

"Besides," Jane continues, "why would I do that to you? You could just as easily expose me if you wanted to."

I nod. She's right. Why would she blackmail me when she's in the exact same position that I am? Besides, she has more than enough money from her fake relationship with Rupert. She doesn't need more from Logan.

I sigh as I collapse onto my bed. I wipe away mascara-stained tears and let myself cry. My chest rises and falls with each sob.

"How could he accuse me of that?" I ask.

Jane sits next to me and pats my back as I cry.

"How could I let myself get so invested in him? How did I let it become so real? I feel like my heart's been ripped out of my chest."

"Oh, Riley." Jane hugs me. "I'm so sorry."

"He cares more about his reputation than anything else. I should have known." I shake my head. "I should have known that a guy like him could never fall for a girl like me."

I bury my face in her shoulder.

"I know, I know." Jane rubs my back. "Damn, I wonder how that blackmailer got that contract."

"I must've left my purse unattended at some point. Maybe in class or at the library." I sigh, annoyed at my own negligence.

"Are you gonna try and figure out who it was?"

"Does it matter?" I slump deeper into the bed. "The damage is done."

"I'm so sorry, Riley."

I look up at her and sigh. "Me too. I guess I can go to New York now, guilt-free."

Jane smiles. "That's the spirit. And you know what else we should do guilt-free?"

"What?"

"Ice cream. Come on, my treat."

I shake my head. "I feel like death. No, worse than death. I feel like a rat that's been through the washing machine."

Jane laughs.

"Trust me," she says. "You'll feel a thousand times better going to get ice cream with me over crying in bed and feeling sorry for yourself. Come on, it closes in fifteen minutes."

After some more convincing on her part, I drag myself out of bed and put on some comfortable jeans and an oversized blue hoodie.

As we walk to the ice cream parlor down the block, I think about everything that happened.

Even though I'm mad at Logan, I want to believe deep down that he didn't mean to accuse me of blackmailing him, or of being unfaithful in this way. But I can still hear his accusations in my head. I can still see the betrayal in his eyes. And even before all that, I could see just how nervous he was to be there upholding his Corazon persona in front of all those journalists. He never cared about me at all.

The stress of it all manifests as a lump in my throat. I try to push it down with a few scoops of mint chocolate chip, but even the ice cream can't numb the pain.

***

"Just this way," Clara, the smartly dressed blond, leads the way through the lobby of the New York City lab.

I follow along with ten other interviewees.

"Being hired by us means an extremely competitive salary and two weeks of vacation days to start. We like to treat our researchers with the highest respect we can. That's how we expect to get the best work out of our employees." She smiles. "Let's turn right and take a tour of the atrium."

We follow her through the brightly lit hallways.

"This place is amazing," a short woman next to me says. "I'd love to work here."

Clara points down the hallway. "The cafeteria is just down that way, with some amazing sustainable and plant-based options. Do you guys think you'd like working here?"

Everyone else nods. I force a smile and nod along with them.

As Clara continues talking about the benefits of working at her lab, I stare longingly out the window at the New York City skyline. A part of me feels defeated. I never imagined myself moving away from Seattle but at this point, it's an inevitability, whether I get this position or not.

"Hey, do I know you?" The short woman asks. "You look familiar."

"Oh, it must be a coincidence."

"No…you were dating that hockey player! What was his name? Logan something…"

"Logan Drake," I say. Saying his name feels like saying a dirty word.

"Right! My brother is a *huge* hockey fan."

"Well, we're not dating anymore."

Her face goes solemn. "Oh, I'm so sorry."

"It's fine."

She smiles, the light appearing in her face again. "It's probably for the best, right? Now you can move to the big apple!"

"Yeah." I swallow past the lump in my throat which still hasn't quite gone away.

I've spent the last week hating Logan *so* much. Even just saying his name fills me with anger. How could he rope me into this mess? How could he blame me when it was clearly his psycho ex-girlfriend who messed this all up?

Or at least I think it was Catherine…

She's the only person who was near my unattended purse when the contract was still in my wallet. She's also the only person I know who's vindictive enough to sabotage a relationship. How could it be anyone else?

I sigh. Does it even matter? Even if Logan wasn't blackmailed, we would have had to break up anyway. But that doesn't stop me from thinking about a whole host of alternate scenarios, none of which involve me being single in New York.

The other interviewees and I follow Clara down a corridor to the atrium. The large rounded room is full of plant life, and the stained-glass ceiling tints the sunlight with jewel-toned blues, reds, greens, and yellows. This small paradise separates the hospital and the laboratories.

"We have revolutionary equipment that will be the future of sports medicine," Clara says. "By working here, you will work with experts who will teach you decades of experience. Our labs are fully stocked and ready to be used. With New York's various elite sports teams, there will be several professional teams needing our services."

Clara smiles as she looks at me, clearly excited that I've had experience with sports medicine.

"Well, that's the end of the tour. I'll be interviewing you all individually over the next few days. Anyone want to volunteer to go first?"

Everyone's hands go up but mine.

Later that afternoon after wasting time at the bookstore down the block, I spend three hours with two doctors as they grill me on hypothetical injury scenarios involving soccer players, ballerinas, and even a golfer. On day two, I show off my anatomy skills by performing a dissection of a fetal pig. On the third day, I complete a long-answer test which seems way more intense than anything I had to do in school.

Needless to say, I'm exhausted by the time I get back to the five-star hotel that the hospital put me up in. The room overlooks the city where I can see the baseball diamond, the new hockey arena, and the mega-hospital. The sound of the busy city buzzes below.

As I stand forty floors up, looking out at the world below me, I can't help but feel like something is missing. Everything is perfect on paper–the hospital, the job, the position–yet my gut screaming that something's not right.

I look at my phone. The screen has been blank for days.

The number of times I've almost dialed Logan's number is embarrassing.

I toss my phone onto the hotel bed and stare out at the city in a blank daze.

I'm mad at Logan for so many reasons. I'm mad that he was still so obsessed with the Corazon trophy. I'm mad that he accused me of blackmailing him. But the reason I'm mad at him the most is that I miss him. And I *hate* that I miss him. I hate that I want him here in this swanky hotel with me. I hate that all I want to do is cook a meal with him and play video games together. I hate that I have to turn off my phone because knowing he's not texting me is breaking my soul into pieces.

And, most of all, I hate that I still love him.

25

LOGAN

The Blades are well into the third round of the playoffs and there's pressure pushing down on me from every angle. We've lost three games in a row against the Cleveland Crushers, my old team. If we don't win the next one, we're out of the playoffs. Meanwhile, the media is running with the story of the hockey bad boy who had a very public breakup. My story is all over the internet and there's nothing I can do to get them to stop talking about it. The one bright light in all this is that the contract is still a secret despite my wallet being one million dollars lighter.

Every time I think of Riley, I feel the sting of betrayal piercing my chest.

The worst part about all this is not seeing Riley in the crowd. I have a sick feeling in my gut that I'm going to lose the playoffs, the Corazon, and Riley all in a few short weeks.

It's game four and our life in these playoffs is on the line. Coach gives us a pep talk but my heart is not in it. Still, I have to push through and be there for my guys.

The puck drops and I'm fighting for it. The crowd is a wave of blue and they're cheering but I can barely hear them. All I focus on is the game at hand. We're already down two goals and time is running out.

Pushing the other team's defenseman against the boards, I get the puck on my stick. Looking up, I see Marcus. I instinctively pass it to him and he takes a shot. Blocked. I get the rebound and shoot right on target. The goalie blocks that one too and the play is whistled down.

Sighing, I instinctively look up into the stands at the family area. Riley isn't there. I focus back on the ice.

As I get ready for another face-off, I note that Cooper is directly in front of me, looking directly into my eyes. I can feel the competitive heat coming off him. For a moment, I'm transported back to our childhood, to those friendly pick-up games at the end of the street.

The referee drops the puck. I pull it away from under him and take a shot, straight off the draw. The goalie gloves it with ease. The buzzer goes off, signaling the end of the second period. I lean over on my knees and shake my head.

"Damn."

Marcus bumps into me. "Don't worry, you'll get one next period."

"I've completely lost my luck," I say.

"You're Logan Drake. You don't need luck."

I look back at the empty seat in the stands.

"You feelin' alright?" Marcus asks. "You look like shit."

"Gee, thanks."

"Seriously though, you seem rough."

"Just frustrated."

As we skate across the ice to make our way to the locker room, he looks at me.

"It's her, isn't it?" He asks. "She really got to you, huh?"

I don't say anything.

"Don't worry about her," he says. "If she doesn't want you, that's her loss."

"Yeah," I agree absently.

"Trust me. If she wanted you, she'd be with you. There's no use in crying over someone who doesn't want you."

"Thanks," I mumble. A horrible public breakup seems to make everyone a relationship expert. Even the wives and girlfriends have been giving me unsolicited advice. All I can do is smile and nod, pretending that their advice will do me good.

As we make our way into the locker room, I find my cubby. As I take my gloves off and toss them aside, I look through my bag for a towel. Something gold catches my eye. Riley's rose pendant necklace.

A knot forms in my stomach. Squeezing my eyes shut, I push away all the memories. I can't let this get to me, not right now. But the simple reminder is enough to send my feelings of self-loathing into a downward spiral.

How could I be such an idiot?

This whole thing was a mistake from the beginning. Why did we have to make that contract? Why did I have to accuse her of something that, deep down, I know she didn't mean to do.

So, how did it happen?

"Drake!" Coach Murphy yells.

I stand up. "Yes, Coach?"

"Where's your mind at right now?"

"It's on the ice, Coach."

"That's not what it looks like. You're capable of more, you hear me? No more distractions."

"Yes, Coach."

"Five more minutes," he says. "Then I want to see all of you play the best twenty minutes of hockey of your damn lives."

"Yes, Coach," the team says.

Marcus furrows his brow as he looks at me. "You gonna be okay?"

"I just need to get some air."

"K, but be quick. We've got some hockey to play."

I cross the locker room and exit out into the hallway where it's cooler, quieter.

There's movement and a bright light to my right. I look up to see several cameras and a journalist interviewing Harrison Cooper. Although I've done my best to avoid him off the ice, moments like this have continually popped up during the last few games.

I turn away, making sure I'm not in the shot. Phone in hand, I want to text Riley and ask her if she's watching, but I avoid it as I've taught myself to do. The background on my phone's home screen is the picture she took that night at the bar. I find myself staring at it often. I can't bring myself to change it. Just seeing her sweet smile and gray eyes remind me how much I love her, how much I miss her.

Shaking my head, I look away.

A tall shadow passes by. It's Cooper.

"Hey Coop," I say. "Good playing out there."

"Oh," he says, surprised that I'm talking to him. "You too. You really found your place on that team."

I give a half-hearted smirk. "They've been good to me."

There's an awkward pause.

"Listen," he says, "about our altercation…"

I put up my hand. "We don't have to talk about that."

"No, we do," he says. "I really liked Catherine and I didn't know what to believe at the time, I—" He rubs his face.

"I know. I'm sorry."

"No," Cooper says. He looks up into my eyes. "I pushed you away from our friendship, our team. It was wrong."

I give him a tight-lipped smile. "Thanks."

"Friends?" He puts his hand out.

"Get in here." I grab Coop's hand and bring him in for a hug.

"Let's grab a drink together after this series is over."

"As long as you promise not to take any nude pictures of me," I say.

We laugh.

"Don't worry," he says. "I have no desire to."

I smirk. "I won't take that personally."

Coop exhales as if he's been holding in a breath for hours. "It's good to be back, bud.'

"Agreed. Good to be back."

He squeezes my shoulder and an overwhelming sense of relief floods through me like I'm relaxing for the first time in a long time.

Coop smirks. "May the best team win."

"May the best team win."

We shake hands before returning to our respective locker rooms. I feel like a weight has been lifted off my shoulders. Marcus playfully punches my shoulder.

"Looks like the fresh air has done you good."

I nod and smile. "I think so. I think things are going to be okay."

If I don't have Riley, at least I still have the lessons she taught me.

"Good," Marcus says. "Because we've got the most important twenty minutes of our lives coming up. Twenty minutes on the ice will turn your mood around. Are you ready to win this thing?"

"I'm ready to give it all I've got."

The next twenty minutes of regulation hockey end up being the craziest twenty minutes of my career. Well, second craziest (the fight on the ice with Coop still takes the cake).

Marcus and I have four shots which are so close that the game has to stop for slow-mo replays. We manage to tie the game up until the last twenty seconds when Coop scores and the Crushers win the game.

The Blades lose.

As the Crushers celebrate, the Blades express their exasperation and frustration.

The defeat washes over me and I feel…fine. As the other guys are slamming their sticks on the ice and burying their faces in their hands, I can't help but feel joyful for my friend and my former team. I feel a great sense of relief knowing that the pressure is no longer on me to perform. I can finally relax.

As Coop skates by me, I smile and give him a fist-bump.

"Good game," I say. "It looks like you'll be buying those drinks."

He smiles gleefully as I pat him on the back.

As he skates away, Marcus skates up next to me.

"Maybe next year." He pats me on the shoulder.

"Yeah," I say. "Although this wasn't so bad."

"We were so close to being amazing."

I squeeze his shoulder. "We *were* amazing."

Marcus smirks. "And we still are"

***

After a long day of press conferences where I spend the day answering questions about the same three topics (the playoffs, the tie with Coop, and potentially winning the Corazon trophy), I finally get on a plane and head back to Seattle.

The sun is already setting when I get to my dark and empty apartment. The place feels larger and quieter than it did before. There's no purse next to the door, no books strewn over the coffee table, no delicious scented strawberry lip gloss or green apple shampoo in the bathroom.

Once I settle back in, I wipe the dust off the surface of the stove and make a meal for one. Sitting on the couch, I watch TV while I eat alone. Back to the status quo.

As I eat dinner, I look up at the shelves on the walls. There are more trophies than I remember–trophies from the juniors, my first year in the international league, and even trophies from when I was a kid. I've been so preoccupied with the empty spot in the middle that I've been ignoring the rest of my achievements. I've been rewarded handsomely for my efforts yet I've always wanted more. And for what? To inflate my own ego? To become an idol?

As I look up at that empty space reserved for the Corazon trophy, I don't feel that longing anymore. I don't feel that impossible standard that I need to live up to.

Riley was right. I don't need any of those things. What I needed was that moment with Coop, to get my friend back. And I did it.

When I'm done my dinner, I retrieve the framed photo of Coop and me from our childhood and I place it in the empty spot on the shelf.

There. No more empty spots. Except for the one that aches in my chest.

Pulling my phone out, I instinctively open my gallery and look at the selfies I took with Riley. I zoom in on her face, her smile, those gray sea-glass eyes.

I'm an idiot. A huge fucking idiot.

Thinking back to the party for Coach, I remember Riley's reaction when I accused her of blackmailing me.

I fucked up. *Bad.*

All Riley ever wanted was for me to find what truly made me happy – not trophies or titles, but friends and girlfriends. No, not girlfriends. Just one. *The* one.

I shake my head.

How could Riley ever want to be near me again after what I accused her of?

Why did I do that? I should have known she'd never betray me. *I should have known.*

But how was I supposed to know? She was the only one with the contract. It was someone close to her who did this. But who, if not her?

I sigh as I sink into the couch.

I was an asshole.

I *am* an asshole.

If only there was some way to let her know that I'd trade the Corazon Trophy away a hundred times just to have things the way they were again. Would she even want me back?

As I stew in my thoughts, I turn on the TV and watch mindless late-night shows as I fall asleep alone.

This is how I spend the next week and a half as I watch the rest of the playoffs to see if Coop and the Crushers win. The only time I peel myself off the couch is when the food delivery guy rings the bell.

When the Crushers win in five games, I feel mixed emotions. I'm happy for my friend and my former team, but I realize just how much I've fallen.

After another few days of self-loathing, I grow tired of throwing myself a pity party. Taking a much-needed shower, I pack up my hockey stuff and drive to the ice rink to release some stress. The cool ice and the sound of the puck hitting the net always helps me clear my mind.

As I step onto the ice, I take in a deep breath of cool air. I do a few laps to warm up before tapping my stick on the ice and taking a shot at the puck.

Usually, hockey is the one way I can disconnect from the world, but today something feels different. My thoughts keep going over all the stupid things I've done, like a supercut of my greatest failures.

Everything I've worked for seems so silly and insignificant now. The Corazon trophy included. All I want is Riley back in my life.

"Who's there?" A deep, boisterous voice echoes.

I look up to see Mr. Balder standing in the stands.

"Hey, Mr. Balder. It's me, Logan. I'm just practicing." I glide to the edge of the rink so we don't have to shout.

"Practicing? It's the post-season! You should be golfing."

"Golfing's not really my sport."

"No shit." He looks me up and down. "You want a ride to the airport?"

"Airport?" I ask, confused.

"Yeah, so we can go to Vegas. The award ceremony is this evening, you dolt!"

"Oh. It is? Are you sure?"

"Yes, I'm sure. And my ride is waiting outside. Are you coming?"

"I—"

I can't believe it. This is the night I've been waiting for all year and now that it's here, I barely care.

"You're going to be a huge star at tonight's ceremony! With the way you played and your reunion with Harrison Cooper. It'd be insane if you didn't go."

I shift my weight uncomfortably from one skate to the other. "I'd have to go home and get my suit."

"You've got time!" Balder waits for my response. "Come on, boy, what are you waiting for?"

"You go ahead, I'll find my own way there."

Balder nods, happy with my compliance. I give him a half-hearted smile.

He pulls away, but not before stopping one last time. "You know, it's too bad you and Riley broke up. You two really had something."

There it is, that aching in my chest comes back like a roaring fire.

"Yeah," I manage to say.

"It's too bad she turned down my job offer. It's not like you two would've been working together that often."

"Wait…what?"

"Riley. I was so impressed with all the projects she was working on at school – you know, we emailed a few times back and forth. I offered her a position working with the medical team. They're opening their own innovative sports medicine lab right here in the city. She was extremely appreciative and, frankly, I thought she'd take it in a heartbeat…but she turned it down because she didn't want to work with you after what happened."

"You offered her a job?"

"Yeah, about a week ago after our season ended. Students always have the best insight into the latest technology. I offered her a good starting salary, benefits and all."

"And she turned it down because of me?"

"She said working with you would hurt too much."

She's turning down her one chance to work in this city because of me?

Guilt floods through my belly.

"Anyway," Balder pats his pockets. "I should go. My ride is waiting but my flight won't. See you later this evening in Vegas. You better be looking good."

"Huh?"

"The awards tonight? You better fuckin' be there. Focus, kid."

"Oh yeah, sure." My mind is elsewhere.

Balder disappears down the hallway.

I stand on the ice in deep thought before deciding to give up for the day. My mind is too distracted.

Heading to the locker room, I shower and change into fresh clothes. As I shove my workout clothes into my gym bag, I spot something shiny pooled at the bottom. It's Riley's rose pendant.

Lifting the necklace up, I admire it as it glitters in the light. Handling it carefully, I put it back into my pocket.

Grabbing my bag, I head out to my car and make a phone call as I hit the road.

"Hello?"

"Mr. Balder? It's me again."

"What now? You better be on your way to the airport, kid."

"I have a favor to ask of you."

Missing the exit for my apartment, I head to the university instead.

26

RILEY

The dorm room is full of boxes as Jane and I pack our last few things.

"I can't believe it," she says, looking around at what used to be our room. "By tonight we'll both be out of here. We'll no longer be students or roommates. Crazy, huh?"

"Crazy. And sad."

"I know." Jane sits on one of the boxes. "I'll miss this place."

I look around at the chipped paint, the old radiator, and the small bed. Even though the aesthetics aren't pleasing, they remind me of so many memories. I think about Logan showing up with apple strudel. I think about all the times I interrupted my studies to watch him play on my tiny laptop screen. I think about all the nights I stayed up late texting with him.

"I'm going to miss this place too," I say.

"That said, I'm *so* excited to live in my luxury apartment downtown and work at Empire Journal as their only new hire this year. Can you believe it? What a dream!" She springs across the room and hugs me, nearly knocking me over. "I'm going to miss you so much."

I hug her back. "I'll miss you too."

It feels good to be missed by someone. These last few weeks have gone by so slowly without Logan. I couldn't help but constantly wonder what he was doing, and if he was thinking about me.

Just thinking about the Blades being swept in the third round makes my heart ache. Logan worked so hard to get to those playoffs and for him to lose when he was so close to the end makes me feel some kind of way. On the other hand, I feel evil for thinking that this is some sort of karma for how everything went down between us.

I gather my luggage and sweep the room one more time to make sure I didn't miss anything. The only thing that's still in the room is the painting that Logan bought for me the first time we went out. I debate leaving it behind for someone else to take. It's just a painful memory that will follow me around. But I reconsider and decide to take it with me. If anything, I can sell it and use the money on a new New York City wardrobe.

"Are you excited to move to the big apple?" Jane asks.

I got the offer to work at the huge hospital and lab a few days after the interviews and I've been in a frantic mood trying to organize everything in time for the big move.

"Yes," I say, without any sort of emotion behind it.

Jane raises an eyebrow. "Are you sure? That didn't sound too convincing."

I sigh. "I just wish the job was here, you know? I don't want to move away."

"Oh honey," Jane hugs me again. "We can still video chat. And you can come and visit me whenever you want. I'll always have a bed for you."

I smile. 'Thanks. You might regret that because I'll take you up on that more often than you realize."

She laughs. "You better!"

After saying our last goodbyes, I gather my stuff and make my way to the student lounge as I wait for my ride to the airport.

Whoever was in the student lounge last left the TV on the sports channel. The countdown is on for the hockey awards. Only a few hours left. Part of me wants to stay and watch, to see if Logan wins, but the stress in my jaw and chest pushes down with full force when I think about it.

Was any of it real?

Did he ever love me?

Questions pop up faster than I can answer them, even more so since Mr. Balder offered me a job with the Blades. I had to say no. There was no way I could ever face Logan again, especially not on a daily basis. Breathing deeply, I pace back and forth to release the pent-up energy that's threatening to take over me.

Ten minutes until my ride arrives. Ten minutes and I'll be off to the airport where I won't have to think about this anymore. Leaving my stuff in the student lounge, I go to the washroom to splash cold water on my face.

"What do I do?" I ask myself in the mirror.

I'm a medical intern now. A New Yorker. There will be plenty of other men to date in New York City, plenty of guys who can wash away the memory of Logan.

I shake my head. My self-reassurances aren't helping. All I want to do is call Logan and leave a really long, embarrassing voice-mail.

Oh *god,* how am I this obsessed with him?

Five minutes until my ride is here.

Heading back to the student lounge, I grab my bags and try to push away the memories I made in this place. I exhale sharply.

"Time for a new start," I remind myself.

But I don't want a new start, my subconscious tells me. *I want to stay here.*

Stepping out into the hallway, I'm momentarily stunned to see a familiar silhouette standing in the hallway. My heart squeezes in my chest.

"Logan?"

He turns around. His face softens. "Riley."

He looks as handsome as ever even though I'm having trouble looking him in the eye.

"What are you doing here?" I'm looking everywhere but him. It hurts too much.

"I came to see you, to give you this."

He holds out my rose pendant necklace.

"Oh." I swallow past the lump in my throat. "Thanks."

Taking the necklace, I hold it in my hand.

"It's been weird not having it."

I finally look up into his eyes. Those beautiful dark eyes that enchanted me so many times in the past. It's hard to look directly at them but, right now, I'm mesmerized. I haven't looked at him in such a long time.

I realize I'm staring a bit too long as I pull my gaze away.

"It didn't bring you too much luck, did it?" I ask as I fasten the necklace around my neck.

He lets out a soft laugh. "I think its magic only works for you."

Letting my defiance slip, I smile for a second before going stone-faced again.

"Is that it?" I ask, straightening my posture. I secure my grip on my bags and the painting.

"No." He steps closer. "I heard Balder offered you a position."

I hold my chin high. "Yeah, so?"

"And you turned it down."

"That's right. I got a position in New York."

"I heard. Congratulations." He sounds sincere.

"Thanks. Well…my ride should be here any minute so I should go."

Holding my stuff tight in my hands, I try to push past him for a dignified and cool-looking exit (as cool as one can look while holding two armfuls of luggage). But Logan steps in front of me, blocking the way.

"*Excuse* me," I say.

"Riley, please just give me a few minutes to get these words out."

I look up at him.

"Riley, I know how much you want to work in Seattle and I know you love the Blades. Balder told me today that the offer is still there if you want it—"

"—Logan, I can't—"

"—I'll leave the team if I make you uncomfortable. I don't want to be the reason you miss out on a dream job in your dream city."

My mouth hangs open with shock. I look into his eyes. "You would leave the team for me?"

He nods. "Seattle's great, but I wouldn't be able to live with myself knowing that you left your home city because of me."

"Wow, Logan. I'm shocked." I'm at a momentary loss for words. "As a Blades fan, I have to ask, where would you go?"

He shrugs. "Alabama's been interested in me for a while. It wouldn't be too hard to get traded considering their team's a mess right now."

"I—I don't know what to say. My ride is downstairs. I'm supposed to be going to New York City."

"They'll find someone else. I know you want to work here in Seattle and I know you love the Blades. Say yes to the job. Stay here. I know it's your legacy to stay here and make your aunt proud."

I look into his eyes. "Why are you doing this for me?"

He takes a step closer.

"I pushed you away," he says. "When I saw that text, I panicked. You were talking about the contract just before that and my mind went to a dark place. You have to understand that I'm so used to being used and hurt and manipulated by past girlfriends that I thought it was happening again."

He lets out a heavy sigh and rubs his face.

"I should have known better."

I look up into his eyes. "I didn't do it. And neither did Jane. I never showed her the contract."

"I know."

"How?"

He shakes his head. "I just know, you know? Deep down I knew you'd never share the contract intentionally. You're too much of a goody two-shoes for that. And I know you're not a greedy person, so there was no reason for you to blackmail me for money. And besides, nude pictures get way more cash. You could have easily taken advantage of me there."

I smirk. "Maybe yours have depreciated in value. It's not like naked photos of you are rare."

He laughs. "Okay, okay. I see you still like to bust my chops."

"I've missed doing that." I smile at him, feeling that spark between us again. When the moment lingers a little too long, I look down at my shoes. "I should have been more careful with the contract. I thought I had it on me at all times. At least, I usually do. But I guess I left my wallet in my purse during one of the games. I'd always run to the concession stand during the second period." I pause. "No, that doesn't make sense. I always brought my wallet with me."

I collect my thoughts for a moment.

"How the hell did the contract get out of my wallet and into someone else's hands?" I wonder out loud.

"It doesn't matter," Logan says. "What's done is done. I'm just glad I was able to catch you before you left."

There's more tension between us.

"I'm so sorry for accusing you, Riley. It's been eating me up inside." His tone is sincere and vulnerable.

"Thanks," I say. "You know, I already knew I'd be moving away that night, the night we broke up. I didn't have any more prospects in Seattle. And you kept talking about the Corazon. I was confused. That's why I was bringing up the contract. I liked our relationship and I wanted to know if what we had was real or not."

I look up into his dark eyes. His expression is unreadable.

"It was real to me," he finally says. His deep voice sends a chill down my spine.

"Oh," I say. "I see."

"I still wanted the trophy. But I was more excited to be there with you that night. I just remember missing you so bad and wanting to dance with you in my arms. I guess I got cocky and tried to have both. Now look at me."

Memories of that strange night flood back before something dawns on me. "Wait a minute… aren't you supposed to be in Las Vegas right now? The award show starts in a few hours! You could still win the Corazon trophy!"

He checks his watch. "My flight should be leaving any minute but it doesn't matter. I don't care about trophies anymore. What matters is you and what you mean to me. I don't want you missing out on a huge opportunity because you hate me. I'd hate me too. That's why you should take the job."

I shake my head in disbelief. "I can't believe you're missing the award show to tell me all this."

"When we broke up, I realized that trophies mean nothing. You taught me that there's so much more to life than just a trophy or a competition. Without you, I wouldn't have made up with Coop. You made me a better man. You changed me."

"Why are you saying all these things?" Tears are threatening to sting my eyes. I do everything I can to hold them back. "Why now?"

He shakes his head. "I don't know, I don't know. I just can't hold it in any longer. And I know you probably hate me, deservedly so. It killed me to play hockey knowing you weren't in the stands watching me, that you weren't sleeping in bed when I got home at night. And it sucks that we'll be living so far away from each other, but I'd rest better at night knowing you're happy doing what you love, knowing that you don't hate my guts. Not completely, at least."

Unsure what to say, I remain silent as I stare at him. My phone buzzes and I know it means that my ride is waiting outside.

Logan touches his chest. "You can hate me all you want, but I need you to know that I love you. I couldn't let you leave without telling you that. I love you, Riley. I love you."

The ache in my chest tightens. Such simple words, yet they do a world of difference. I swallow back the emotion that's forming in my throat.

He's missing the award show. He wants to move away for me.

The gesture is overwhelming.

"Logan—" I look up into his eyes. "I don't hate you."

His eyebrows raise, his lips turn into a slight smile. For a moment, I forget we're in a university dorm hallway. Luckily, the sound of the student lounge microwave starts humming in the other room to remind us.

"Oh hey," a nasal voice behind me says.

I turn around to see Keith standing in the student lounge doorway. He's wearing a fitted pair of jeans and a crisp white button-down with blue paisley cuffs. His hair is cut and styled. He looks like a completely different person.

"Keith, can you give us a moment?" I ask.

Keith steps out into the hallway and I can just tell that he wants to annoy me one last time. But when he spots Logan, his expression changes.

"Oh, my bad." Keith retreats back into the student lounge.

That's weird, I think. Keith rarely backs off so easily.

"Wait," Logan says in a commanding voice. Keith stops in the doorway and turns around. Logan squares his shoulders so that he's staring straight at Keith who looks frozen in place.

"Yes?" Keith asks sheepishly.

"Where did you get those clothes?" Logan asks.

I look at Logan with a raised eyebrow. *What the hell is he doing asking Keith about his clothes?*

Keith looks down at his outfit and shrugs.

"The store?" He gives Logan a timid shit-eating grin.

"That's a three-hundred-dollar shirt," Logan says. "Where'd you get the money for that?"

Keith swallows.

"Well, I got a job with a popular journal downtown."

"Really?" I ask. "Where?"

"Um, it's called Empire Journal."

"No, you didn't," I say. "They only had one open position this summer and Jane got it."

The microwave in the student lounge starts beeping.

"Oh, I—" He stutters as he backs away into the student lounge. "My meal is ready, I should go—"

Logan points his finger. "You're the one who messaged me. You're the piece of shit who blackmailed me!"

Keith freezes in place and puts his hands up. "I have no clue what you're talking about."

His cheeks turn bright red.

I instantly bring my hands to my mouth. "Is it true?"

"You two sound crazy." Keith waves us off. "I didn't do anything."

"Yes, you did," Logan says. "At the student bar when Riley and I first started dating. Riley was in the washroom. You looked through her purse because you wanted change for the jukebox."

"Oh my god." My eyes grow wide.

The contract was in my wallet. If Keith was rifling through my wallet for change, he *definitely* saw it.

"Listen, I don't know what you're talking about." Beads of sweat are now forming on Keith's pale brow. He looks exactly like a man who has just been exposed.

"This is what's going to happen," Logan says as he breathes in and takes a step forward, turning his intimidation factor up to a hundred. "You're going to turn on your phone right now and you're going to delete all the copies of that image. And you're going to return the money too."

A thrill runs through me. There's something incredibly sexy about Logan giving orders.

"You want me to give back the money?" Keith has an annoyed and crazed look in his eye.

"I can't fucking believe it," I say. "Actually, scratch that. I absolutely can believe this. What the fuck, Keith?"

"I never meant to hurt you, Riley. Please don't hold this against me."

I roll my eyes. "Open your damn phone."

"And if I don't?"

Logan takes another step forward. "If you don't, I'll have an army of lawyers suing your ass for the invasion of Riley's privacy. I'll tell Empire Journal that you were posing as one of their journalists and that you used invasion of privacy and blackmail to get a story. This will quietly get you blackballed from Seattle's entire journalism industry. In addition to losing your career, you'd owe us millions of dollars, more than you already owe me. Is that a risk you really want to take?"

His voice is low, threatening, and (frankly) extremely sexy.

Keith is squirming uncomfortably in place. I can't help but smile.

"Fine." Keith pouts.

He pulls his phone out and navigates to the picture of the contract. He selects the delete button.

"There," he sneers. "Are you happy?"

"And our chat too," Logan says.

Keith navigates to their chat history and empties the gallery, as well as any copies in the cloud.

"Good," Logan says. "Now, about the money…"

Keith sighs.

"I can wire it to you tonight." His voice is rife with dejection.

"No, I don't want it. You'll send it as a donation to the biomechanics lab at this university. You'll say it's an anonymous donation in honor of Mary Jamieson."

I whip around to look at Logan, giving him a surprised but appreciative smile. He smiles back and my heart softens.

"Fine," Keith mumbles as he shoves the phone into his pocket. "I'm glad I never have to see you two again."

"Likewise," I say.

"And you," Keith looks up at Logan, "I hope you lose tonight."

"Stay classy," Logan says as Keith disappears back into the student lounge.

Logan's eyes connect with mine.

"Oh my god," I say. "I can't believe that just happened!"

"I knew there was something wrong with that guy."

"We all did, frankly." I smile. "Thank you. I'm just…wow, I'm shocked."

Logan runs his hands through his hair. "I wasn't expecting that today."

Our eyes lock. An awkward silence forms between us.

"Riley, I'm so sorry for everything. I blamed you for this and, in the end, it was my fault. If I actually did my job that night and watched your purse, none of this would have happened. Deep down, I knew you didn't do that to me. I was stupid to assume you did."

I smile as I look down at my feet.

"Yeah, well…we all make mistakes, don't we?"

I look up and smirk at him.

"Can I help you with your bags? It's the least I can do."

I nod, feeling a sinking feeling in my belly as I realize I's still supposed to be going to New York.

He takes my suitcases and I take the painting as I lead the way out of the dorm building for the last time. We walk through the hallway and down the stairs until we're outside. It's a beautiful sunny day.

I stop and look up into his eyes.

"Thank you for donating that money to the school," I say.

He nods. "It seemed like the right thing to do."

There's awkward energy between us.

"Riley, I feel really bad right now. I understand if you never want to see me again. As I said, the offer for the job is still up so if you want it—"

"—I do," I say.

"Oh." This catches him by surprise. "Okay, great. Umm, do you have Balder's number? Because if you don't, I can give it to you—"

I hold my hand up.

"Logan, stop." I take a step closer to him. He smells so good, like he just got out of the shower. "I want the job. But I also think you should stay with the Blades too. You clearly click with the team. You should stay if you want to. Because I want you to."

His lips slowly curl into a smile.

"You wouldn't mind seeing me around?" He asks as he tilts his head to the side and squints in the sun. "Like co-workers, or friends?"

"Or maybe something more than friends."

He smiles. "Is that really how you feel?"

I nod. "I never stopped feeling that way."

"So, would it be okay if I did this?" He reaches for my hand, brushing his fingertips against mine.

I smile.

Noting my reaction, he takes my hand in his, interlacing our fingers together. A surge of warmth flows through me. I forgot just how comforting he feels. In an instant, the lump in my throat disappears.

"I missed you," he says, his low voice vibrating deep in his throat.

"I missed you *so* much," I say. "The number of times I wanted to call and text you… I had to hide my phone from myself."

He lets out a soft laugh as he pushes the hair out of my face. Our lips get closer as I stare into his eyes.

"I'm so sorry about the playoffs," I whisper.

He shrugs. "It's just a game. I realized over these past few weeks that there are way more important things in life."

My eyes flash down to his lips. Those beautiful, plump lips. I look back up into his eyes.

"Logan—I love you, and I'm in love with you… I'm in love with you *so* much."

He lets out a gentle laugh. "Is that a thing people say?"

"It's a thing I say."

He smirks. "I'm in love with you so much too, Riley."

Pulling me close, he kisses me. The kiss is like a breath of fresh air after being underwater for too long. Wrapping my arms around his shoulders, I melt into his body as if there's a space carved out just for me.

His hand finds its way into my hair as he kisses me so softly, so sweetly, that I can feel just how much he's been longing to do it.

He strokes my face gently.

"I love you," he whispers.

"I love you too."

We kiss again, not caring that we're standing out on campus in front of everyone. They can watch all they want.

When we finally emerge from several weeks of missed kisses, we laugh.

"I've been dreaming of doing that," he says.

I suppress a smile. "Me too."

His fingers caress mine. "So, do you want to go on a date with me? Maybe we can get some dinner."

"Sure." I give him a devilish smile. "But only if I get to choose where."

Logan smiles before kissing me again.

"Your wish is my command."

27

RILEY

Two and a half hours later we're in Las Vegas.

We manage to make it to the award show fashionably late in outfits we changed into on the airplane ride there. We both look surprisingly glamorous considering we had to pull outfits out of our overhead luggage and change in the tiny airplane bathrooms.

Luckily, Jane gave me a white cocktail dress which she told me was essential for New York City nightlife. Hopefully it translates to Las Vegas glam too.

When we finally make it to the Las Vegas strip, the award ceremony is half over. Luckily, we get there just in time for the presentation of the Corazon trophy. We have just enough time to find our seats before the next presenter makes his way on stage.

We're seated next to the captain, Rory Edgar, who is wearing a dapper gray suit with a blue tie that matches his stunning blue eyes. The goalie, Skip McGovern, is wearing a cool leather jacket and a bolo tie. His red hair is up in a man bun. Marsha, his bubbly blond girlfriend, is seated next to him in a sparkly light pink dress. She waves at me excitedly as we sit down. We have just enough time to get settled before the winner is called.

I look over at Logan.

"Whatever happens," I say, "I'm proud of you."

He smiles and squeezes my hand. "I don't need a trophy. I have everything I need right here."

"And the winner is Harrison Cooper!" The announcer calls out. The crowd erupts into applause, including Logan. In fact, he's the first person to stand up, whistling and hollering as he does so.

When he sits back down, I look over at him and squeeze his hand.

"I'm happy for him," Logan says. "He deserves it."

And I can tell he's telling the truth. I don't see sadness or regret in his eyes, only appreciation for his friend.

"Wow, thanks," Cooper says as he approaches the microphone. He's looking at the trophy in awe. "This is amazing! Thanks to the Crushers and Coach Brauer. Playing with you guys has been a dream, I couldn't have done this without you. And there's someone else I couldn't have done this without. That's, of course, my best friend who keeps me honest on the ice. Logan, I wouldn't have won this if you didn't push me to be competitive. I'm glad we're friends again, buddy."

After Coop finishes his speech, he walks off stage and I can tell Logan wants to get up and go congratulate him. I have to hold him back, reminding him that the ceremony is still going. The next trophy is already being announced.

An old man is standing on stage. "The winner of the Gentleman's Trophy will go to the player who showed great sportsmanship both on and off the ice. The winner this year is someone who built bridges, held on to friendships, and handled difficult losses with grace. The winner this year is Logan Drake."

"What?" He looks around in confusion.

"You won!" I shake him. "The Gentleman's Trophy. It's yours!"

Everyone is clapping and looking at us. Logan looks absolutely shocked. He gets up slowly, as if still expecting it to be a joke but it's not. Rory and Skip lean over to shake his hand as he gets up. In shock, he makes his way up to the stage to thunderous applause as he takes the trophy in his hands.

"Wow," he says into the microphone. "Thank you so much, I didn't expect this. Are you sure this isn't a mistake? I mean, I fought with my own player this season."

The crowd laughs. The old man who handed him the trophy rushes up to the microphone and says, "You made up with him too." The crowd cheers again.

"Yeah," Logan says. "I guess that's true. Our friendship can outlast any on-ice fight. I guess I'll thank Coop for always starting fights with me, ever since we were kids. I'll thank the Crushers for kicking me off their team, and the Blades for taking me in. And I'd like to thank one last person, a special person who taught me that kindness always wins out. Thank you, Riley."

I'm holding my hand on my heart as I watch him. My eyes are swimming with happy tears.

The award is the huge upset of the night. After the ceremony, Logan and I spend an hour talking to the other guys. Eventually Coop comes out and they find each other.

As I watch Logan congratulating Coop and laughing with him, I truly believe the trophy is not even the second or third most important part of his night.

"He did good," Rory says. His large stature and intense stare are quite intimidating. I understand why he's the captain.

"Yeah," I say. "Thanks for being such a good captain for him. He really needed that this year."

Rory smirks. "It's just my job."

"Hey." Connor Saito comes up to us as he taps on his phone. "Have you heard about this new prospect for next year's team? Jack Lalonde? Coach says he's going to draft him."

"Yeah, he's some French-Canadian up-and-comer with hot hands," Rory says. "He's supposed to be really good."

"I call dibs on mentoring him. Daisy will be gone all year so I'll need someone around the house."

Rory laughs. "Being a mentor doesn't mean making him do your laundry."

"I know that!"

The guys continue chatting about next year's new prospects as I watch Logan and Coop laugh and chat with each other. Walking up to them, I congratulate Coop.

"Thanks for straightening this guy out," Coop says. He looks handsome in a blue suit with a skinny black tie.

I smile. "I think he deserves just as much credit for that than I do."

Coop laughs. "I don't know… he was pretty hopeless before you."

I smirk as I look over at Logan.

He nods. "It's true."

I laugh as the press comes over and begs us for photos. The press is very interested in the fact that we're together again, but not as interested as they are in Logan's relationship with Coop. Logan holds me close as they snap some photos.

A few celebratory shots later, Logan holds his trophy in one hand as he pulls me through the Bellagio hotel lobby with the other.

Although we spent a good chunk of the flight to Vegas making up for all the conversation and life updates we missed out on, I'm ready for something a bit more physical.

Giggling like teenagers, I pull him into the elevator, ready to push him against the wall and play some tonsil hockey with him. He stops me before I get too handsy as we notice an older woman standing in the elevator with us. She's wearing a yellow visor and a neon green fanny pack.

We both give her a tight smile as we try to hold in our laughter.

"What did you win?" The old lady asks, looking at the trophy.

Logan holds his trophy up. "The Gentleman's Trophy. It's for sportsmanship and gentlemanly conduct, along with a high standard of playing ability."

"Oh! Well, you must be quite the gentleman." Her face wrinkles as she smiles. The elevator pings and she wishes us a good evening before shuffling off.

When the doors close, I place my hands on Logan's chest again. He smells like woodsy cologne and a fine pressed suit.

"Gentlemanly conduct," I whisper into his ear. "I wonder what it's like to spend the night with hockey's most esteemed gentleman."

He smirks.

"Lucky me," he says in his low, rolling voice. "Why don't I show you?" He presses forward, kissing me confidently on the lips. I melt against his kiss as heat rushes through my body.

The elevator pings again and he pulls me into the Grand Lakeview Suite.

The first thing I see when I walk in is hot pink decor with pear-green accents. The striped chairs, the floral carpet, and the metallic curtains all share the same energetic and opulent colors.

"Look at this place!" For a moment I'm distracted as I break away from Logan. Tossing my purse onto the gray velvet couch, I walk over to the large window overlooking the iconic Bellagio Fountains. Water shoots up into the air and dances back and forth.

Logan places the trophy on a nearby table before walking up and standing behind me, sliding his arms around my waist.

"The view's more beautiful with you here." He kisses my neck. His warm minty breath sends chills over my skin.

I turn around and look up into his dark eyes. I kiss him again, slowly, savoring the way he feels, the way he tastes.

"Come," he says. "Let me show you the rest of the suite."

Kissing me again, he lifts me effortlessly and carries me to the bedroom before placing me on the king-sized bed. Placing his warm hands on my body, he pulls my white cocktail dress down off my body and tosses it aside before peeling off his jacket, loosening his tie, and unbuttoning his shirt.

Once he tosses those aside, he joins me on the bed. His lips find my neck and slowly move down as he begins kissing me everywhere. I arch my back, melting into the softness of his lips

"I've missed you," I whisper. *"Logan."*

His soft and messy hair sweeps over my exposed skin, tickling me as his lips move up over my breasts to my neck.

"I'll never let you go," he whispers back. "Never again."

His hands feel like velvet as they touch my skin. His warmth comforts me like a warm blanket. I inhale his masculine woodsy aroma as if wanting to commit it to memory forever. I listen to his deep breathing, feeling his chest rise and fall against mine.

Rocking his body, he pushes into me with that familiar strength and control. He moves slow at first, but as his hands and lips explore me more, he becomes more ravenous. He holds me tight against him as we move more passionately and vigorously than ever before.

I want him. I want *all* of him.

As the bed begins to shake, I moan so loudly that it echoes off the tall walls, causing me to feel slightly concerned for our neighbors down below. Logan and I smile for a moment of levity before getting lost in each other again.

As Logan pushes deeper, I get closer to the edge. With an explosion of pleasure that radiates from my head down to my curled toes, I hold on tight to Logan, pressing my fingernails into his back. A masculine grunt escapes his throat, punctuating his heavy breathing. He tenses every muscle in his body before collapsing onto me. He rests his nose on my hair, breathing me in.

"I love you," he whispers.

I smile as I kiss his salty sweaty forehead and run my hands through his wild hair. “I love you too,” I whisper back.

After having some of the best sex we’ve ever had (twice), we order room service to satiate our ravenous appetites. I order the lobster while Logan gets the steak. After devouring an ungodly amount of food, we shower and get dressed. I put on a black skirt and a silky pink camisole while Logan wears jeans and a crisp black t-shirt.

“Ready for a debaucherous night on the town?” He asks.

“You mean to say that what we just did wasn’t debaucherous?”

He laughs. “Trust me, you haven’t seen anything yet.”

“Your reputation does precede you, Mr. Drake.”

We head downstairs to have fun at the casino. After stopping to say hi to a few other hockey players, Logan and I grab some drinks and walk around, soaking up the glamour and debauchery of sin city.

“To a wonderful hockey season,” I say as I hold up my Long Island Iced Tea. “And to the most gentlemanly man in the league.”

Logan holds up his glass of whiskey. “To my beautiful girlfriend who helped me get there.”

Our glasses clink and we both drink.

“So.” He points at an empty roulette table. “Are you a gambling lady?”

I smirk. “I think you know the answer to that. I gambled on you, didn’t I?”

He smiles as he touches the small of my back as we walk to the roulette table.

"Hello folks, how are you tonight?" The dealer asks. He's an older gentleman with a bald head and an impressive beard.

"Great," I say.

"Ready to do some gamblin'?"

I nod as I place twenty dollars on the table. The dealer exchanges it for a single black chip.

"Where are you going to put it?" Logan asks.

I hold the chip in both hands as I look at the table. "I was thinking number thirteen unless you have a better suggestion?"

He smirks. "Do you want to up the stakes?"

Looking over my shoulder, I give him a flirty stare. "What do you have in mind, Mr. Drake?"

"Well…" He leans against the table, looking like a rebel with a purpose. "Let's say if it lands on black, we get married. Tonight."

My eyes grow wide. *"What?"*

He reaches into his pocket and pulls out a small box.

"Oh my god, Logan—" I bring my hands to my mouth in shock as I look into his eyes. "When did you have the time to get that?"

Seriously, he hasn't left my side since we met at the university earlier today. This could only mean that he's had that this whole time. My heart goes into overdrive.

With a smirk, he opens the box to reveal a ring identical to my Aunt Mary's rose pendant. My hand instinctively touches my necklace.

He holds the open ring box under the light so I can get a better view.

"Is that real?"

He nods. "I've had it since the beginning of the playoffs. I saw that you might be moving to New York and I couldn't stand the thought of not being by your side."

My mouth hangs open as I stare at the ring. The diamonds sparkle under the casino's brilliant lighting.

"Oh, Logan, it's absolutely beautiful."

"So?" He asks. "What do you think?"

I look into his eyes. "I don't know what else to say besides… are you *crazy?*"

He laughs. "A lot of people would say I am."

I look down at the ring again.

He takes my hand and caresses it in his.

"If you think it's crazy, place that chip on red and I'll put that ring back in my pocket. But if you put it on black, then we'll see what fate decides for us. And if fate decides favorably, then you'll bring me more joy than any trophy or cup ever could."

His velvety touch moves up my wrist as his gaze lingers on me. I'm still holding the chip in my hand. My lips curl into a subtle smirk as I look down at the numbers on the table.

"Place your bets!" The dealer says.

Biting my smile, I watch as the dealer spins the wheel.

"Last chance," the dealer says.

I look into Logan's hopeful eyes one last time before placing the chip down on number thirteen. Black.

"Bets are closed," the dealer says. He drops the ball onto the spinning wheel as it rolls around and around making a *tac-tac-tac-tac-tac* noise.

Looking up, I see Logan smiling wider than I've ever seen him smile.

"You put it on black," he says.

I place a hand on his chest. "I'm always going to bet on you, Logan Drake."

Moving closer, he pulls me against him as he lowers his lips to meet mine. He tilts my chin up as he kisses me, causing excitement to bloom inside my belly. There's no crowd of people watching us. There are no smartphones sending pictures to media outlets. There's no contract or trophy to worry about. It's just us. Just Logan and me, the way it should be. And I can't stop smiling.

We're so lost in our own world that we don't even notice the sound of the wheel coming to a stop, nor do we hear the dealer announce the winning color. We know that we've already won.

Thank you for supporting indie authors!

I loved writing this one! The fake boyfriend trope is one of my favorites. If you liked this story, please leave a review and let me know so I can write more like it!

-Violette

Want more? Keep reading...

Jack

(An Opposites Attract Hockey Romance)

Hockey rookie Jack Lalonde is about to start his first year of professional hockey with the Seattle Blades. During his first outing in the new city, he spends a magical night with a bewitching and mysterious woman. Tarot cards, crystals, and a black cat... she might even be a witch. They could not be more opposite... hockey and astrology do not mix. He needs to focus on hockey, but she casts a strong spell and he cannot resist her magic forever.

If you love steamy hockey romance where opposites attract, grab "Jack" and start reading!

Also by Violette Paradis

Bad Boys of Hockey

The Seattle Blades are sexy, rebellious, and always ready to heat up the ice!

Logan - *A Fake Boyfriend Hockey Romance*

Jack - *An Opposites-Attract Hockey Romance*

Rory - *A Second Chance Hockey Romance*

Cooper - *An Opposites Attract Hockey Romance*

Verona - *A Secret Baby Hockey Romance*

Dean - *Boss-Employee Hockey Romance*

Austin - *A Second Chance Brother's Best Friend Hockey Romance*

JACKSONVILLE STALLIONS

Always up for a challenge, the Jacksonville Stallions are hungry to prove themselves.

Rule Breaker - *An Enemies-to-Lovers Hockey Romance*

Icy Temptation - *A Grumpy/Sunshine Single Dad Fake Fiancé Hockey Romance*

Offside Attraction - *A Secret Identity Enemies-to-Lovers Hockey Romance*

Visit www.violetteparadis.com for more

Printed in Great Britain
by Amazon

28297465R00151